Purrfectly Timed

A MAVERICK PRIDE TALE

C.D. GORRI

Purrfectly Timed
A Maverick Pride Tale
by C.D. Gorri
Edited by BookNookNuts

To anyone who has ever waited for love, Don't listen to the critics.
Sometimes, timing is everything.
Happy reading.
Xoxo,
C.D. Gorri

Before you begin, sign up for my newsletter here:
https://www.cdgorri.com/newsletter

Note from the author...

Hello Readers!

Thank you for purchasing this Maverick Pride Tale featuring *Uncle Uzzi's Magical Matchmaking Service* and one of my favorite Golden girls, Antonetta, or Toni for short. We've met this feisty feline a few times, most recently supporting her sister Annabeth in Purrfectly Paired, and helping her other sister, Ariella, out in Pinch of Sass.

If you're thinking this is another series crossover book, you are right! As with some of my other series, my Dire Wolf Mates and Maverick Pride Tales books have often had visits from each other's characters, and I plan to continue on that bend. Hopefully you enjoy it, too.

Toni is such a wonderful character and Pierce is

just purrfect for her. I can't wait for you to see them together. Alright, let's get to Toni and Pierce's story!

Happy reading!

Xoxo,

C.D. Gorri

Blurb

Pierce is on the hunt for someone to call his own, but this kitty throws him for a loop.

Pierce McDowd is surrounded by mated pairs, but he can't find anyone to call his own. His concentration is nil, and the Pride Neta has had it with his mistakes.

It's time to bring in the big guns. Decision made, Pierce sends word to *Uncle Uzzi's Magical Matchmaking Service*. If anyone can help him find his mate, Uncle Uzzi can!

Antonetta Golden is no ordinary Lioness. Labeled trouble by men who could not handle her, this kitty is more than meets the eye. Single and not loving it, she's made her career her focus. But when trouble sprouts at work, Toni is suspended. What can she do besides drive herself crazy?

Trust in Uncle Uzzi to deliver a solution! Purrfect timing didn't exist for this Lioness before, but a weekend getaway to meet the male of her dreams sounds just right.

Find out if Pierce and Toni get their happy ever after in this installation of the Maverick Pride Tales.

Preface

Dark clouds loomed overhead as Uzzi Stregovich opened the sliding glass doors so he could step out onto the terrace of his condo in Maccon city, New Jersey. He'd decided to spend the summer there, as it was one of his favorite spots on the East Coast.

His cup of coffee was full and hot, and all was right with the world. Well, mostly. He missed his wife like crazy, but she was still with him. Even now, he felt her spirit hovering near.

Uzzi greeted her n his head, then took a sip and almost spit it out. Grimacing, he looked into the mug, lifted it, and sniffed.

Richard! That busybody of a housekeeper was sneaking decaf into his cupboard again. Damn the man!

Uzzi knew he was only trying to look after his health. Still, he should know better than to do that to a Witch. He looked around, making sure no one else was about before he waved his hand over his mug, shooting blue sparks as he magicked some caffeine into the brew.

"There now. This is better," Uzzi murmured.

He blew on the hot liquid manna from heaven, heaving a happy sigh. Uzzi sat down at a small wrought iron bistro set that graced the semi-private terrace. It was summer, but the weather had been terrible lately.

This was the first break in the thunderstorms menacing the entire eastern seaboard for the past week. It was killing tourism, but Uzzi was an optimist. It couldn't rain all the time.

The morning air was ripe with ozone from the last shower, but he was grateful it had abated. His ocean view was undisturbed, and even though the sea was rough, it was always something wonderful to behold.

Spotting a few dolphins in the distance, Uzzi smiled. This was exactly what he needed. He wanted to enjoy his coffee and perhaps scroll through his emails. Who knew? Maybe he would have some from one of his many clients.

Catering to supernaturals around the world, and beyond, *Uncle Uzzi's Magical Matchmaking Service* was a veritable household name, well, in certain circles, of course. He'd been doing this an incredibly long time, but it never got old.

Like all Witches, male, female, or other, Uzzi's magic was a craft he practiced daily. And like all crafts, the more time spent on it, the better he got. Even now, he felt that old familiar hum of magic zipping up and down his spine.

The first notice in his email app was from his *Eat Well Live Proud* account. He would have to tell Richard, since he doubled as housekeeper and personal cook, to expect another delivery sometime that week. It was always a thrill to see what goodies the Lion Shifter corporation had in store for him.

The Blue Valley Lion Pride was one of his favorite Shifter groups in the Garden State. Their King had recently claimed a new queen, and all was right with the group, as far as he could tell. Of course, Uzzi had worked matches for two of the Queen's young.

To humans, Shifters were the stuff of legends, as were Witches, but for Uzzi, this was very much his reality. *Eat Well Live Proud* might be just another global conglomerate famous for their farm to table services, but to him, the company and the Lions who ran it were family.

"Now, it has been just a few days since I saw them, so why should I be thinking so much about these pussycats? I do wonder, *liebling*, if the Fates are not playing their games again," he murmured, speaking aloud to his dearly departed Betty.

Being a Witch and matchmaker, not to mention a descendant of the goddess of love, Aphrodite herself, meant Uzzi had learned to trust his *feelings* long ago. Usually, his instincts were spot on.

Therefore, instead of ignoring his thoughts, he allowed them to wander. A small smile played at the corners of his mouth as one Lioness in particular drifted to mind. Antonetta Golden was a favorite of Uzzi's. Bold, brilliant, beautiful. She was a triple threat, and if memory served, still single.

"Interesting," he murmured.

Uzzi continued to scroll and sip while thunder boomed, and lightning lit the sky. It was not raining yet. Good. very good. Uzzi still had a few more minutes of fresh air, he mused.

"Spam. Spam. Trash. Oooh, a book sale! Wait. Hold the phone. *Wunderbar!*" Uzzi enthused as he clicked on the email.

Dear Uncle Uzzi,

It has been a while since you visited Maverick Point, and Hunter and Elissa both agree a visit is long overdue. I am hoping you can spare some time to come see us, well, me in particular. Or I can come to you. Whatever works.

You see, I am having some difficulties with my Tiger, and I need your help. I think the silly cat wants me to find a mate, but Uncle Uzzi, there is no one here who piques my interest.

I have been messing up at work, and Hunter is at his wit's end. He's forcing me to take some time off until I get my head on straight, but my Tiger is being surly as heck. Could I be right? Will a mate settle my inner beast?

So, I guess I am writing to ask you for your help. Is there anything you can do for me?

Thanks again.

Sincerely,

Pierce McDowd of The Maverick Pride

Little sparks of blue magic danced up and down Uzzi's fingers while he re-read the email. Pierce McDowd was a handsome young Tiger Shifter with black hair and aquamarine-colored eyes full of promise and virility.

He was an honest male, hardworking, too. The Neta spoke highly of the young male the last time Uzzi was in town. If memory served, he had just been promoted at Maverick Development and was now taking an active role in managing contracts.

"That's right. He was in law school the last time I was there. Hmmm, looks like he passed the bar," Uzzi murmured.

So Pierce was a lawyer, working for his Pride's firm. A good catch, for sure. But for whom?

That was always the kicker. He took another fortifying sip and closed his eyes allowing his thoughts to process. Suddenly, Uzzi's mind wandered back to a certain dark-haired Lioness just as thunder clapped. He opened his eyes at the same moment the rain started to fall.

"Wunderbar!" Uzzi grinned.

He had a feeling about this one. A good feeling. It just came down to timing.

Prologue

"What the fuck? Pierce! Get your striped ass in here!" Hunter Maverick, Neta of the Maverick Pride, shouted from his office.

Pierce winced. Fuck. Hunter must have gotten the same notice he did about the supplies they needed to finish a job they'd been contracted to complete on some government buildings in downtown Jersey City.

Instead of having the items delivered from their usual supplier, he'd gone with a less known, and apparently less reliable overseas supplier who had royally fucked up. The shipment was lost at sea, tying up tens of thousands of dollars the company could ill afford to waste.

He was hoping to use his own funds to replace the order, in fact, he had already started that process, but it seemed his mistake would not go unnoticed after all. Well, there was no use in delaying the inevitable.

"Here, son," Brayden, the Pride Beta, and a Bear Shifter, handed him an ice pack.

"What's this for?" he asked, walking past a group of the guys who were all getting coffee before heading out.

It wasn't even dawn yet, but they started early at Maverick Development. Hunter liked to see his foremen before they headed out each day. Brayden was their top guy. Pierce should know, he used to work under him.

But after he passed the bar and was now, technically, a lawyer, Hunter had put him to work indoors. He wasn't supposed to handle orders, mostly contracts, and permits and stuff like that.

Reg, the Tiger who usually handled orders, was out with his mate on maternity leave, and Pierce had filled in. Well, he'd tried to fill in, but it was more like he'd fucked up.

Grrr.

"That's to put on your ass, son, after Hunter gets

done chewing you up and spitting you back out," the male replied and grinned.

The rest of the guys laughed, a couple of them giving him slaps on the back as he walked by. Shit. Pierce was in hell. Pure fucking hell.

He shook his head and walked to the Neta's office, knocking first, and waiting for permission before heading in. He was not about to give the male any other reason to give him shit. Lord knew he deserved everything he was going to get.

He rubbed the area in the middle of his chest to ease the dull ache that always seemed to plague him. More and more, Pierce felt as though something was missing from his life. His animal was restless, the seven hundred and fifty pound Bengal Tiger he shared his soul with was a massive beast whose primal urges lately seemed to include daydreaming and fucking up at work.

Fuuuccccccck.

"Look, Hunter, let me start by apologizing for my lack of focus," he began, but the Neta gave him one look through his glowing teal eyes and Pierce shut his mouth.

The male was clearly in no mood. He lowered his gaze, baring his throat to show his respect for the male, and his loyalty to his position as Neta of their

Pride. Tiger Shifters were not like Wolves or Lions, their numbers were miniscule in comparison.

Fealty was everything, and after the recent betrayal of one of their own, it was only natural for Hunter's Tiger to flex his Neta power now and again. Understandable even more, considering the good news. Hunter was going to be a father—*again*. Elissa, their Nari, was expecting another set of cubs. After the birth of their magnificent twins Melly and Celia, the entire Pride was near to bursting with happiness.

Pierce, too. Only with that happiness came a side dish of greenery he was not expecting. Envy was a bitch, and his Tiger chuffed unhappily at the thought he might never experience the same joy that Hunter had.

Not that he wasn't happy for the Neta. The male deserved his happiness. He had certainly earned it. There was no better man for the job of leading their Pride, as he had proven repeatedly. Defeating Blake, that rogue bastard who had tried to hurt them. Securing his line by finding his true love and gifting his mate a Tiger of her own when she underwent the Puspa—a mystical and magical occurrence that only happens when mates are blessed by the Fates themselves.

The Maverick Pride had a lot to be grateful for, and anger surged within him for threatening that which they had worked so hard to gain.

"Sit down, Pierce," Hunter said, his Tiger apparent in the growl of his voice.

He rubbed a hand over his bald head and cocked his head to the side. Pierce's Tiger felt better in his presence, though the need to submit had him bowing his head lower than normal.

Shit. Hunter must be really pissed, he thought.

"What happened? You are one of the smartest males in the Pride, Pierce. It is not usual for you to make mistakes like this," Hunter began diplomatically.

"Apologies, Neta. I have fixed the mistake, on my own dime, as I should."

"That is not necessary—" Hunter began, but Pierce shook his head.

"It is. It was my error, Neta. Please allow me to correct it," he said, and waited.

"You know, I was surprised after you passed the bar that you wanted to stay working for the Pride. I thought maybe you wanted to open a small firm or go to the city. You know, some males as they get older find they can't settle within a Pride—"

"No! I don't want to go rogue. Never that, Neta,"

Pierce interrupted, eyes wide with shock. "I have only ever wanted to be a better Tiger for this Pride. I know I have not been myself, but I think I know why."

"Really? So, what is going on?"

Pierce's Tiger scratched and snarled. Ironic that a man who was the epitome of eloquence in law school was shit at talking to the one male he trusted more than anyone else on the planet. He enjoyed his time at Seton Hall. Didn't even mind the long drive back and forth every day.

But Pierce didn't take the bar to become Matlock or anything. He didn't want to go rogue. Fuck that. His whole life was the Pride.

It was just. Well. Shit.

How the fuck was he supposed to say this? He cleared his throat and rubbed the back of his neck, daring to meet Hunter's stare for a single moment before averting his gaze. The man's power was awesome in every sense of the word, and Pierce was in no way challenging him. He just needed him to know he was baring his fucking soul here.

"It's everyone finding their mates," he confessed. "I mean, my Tiger is restless. He wants a family, but none of our females are right for me. I, uh, I don't know what to do."

"Pierce, my man," Hunter shouted with a laugh. "That is wonderful news! Fuck, bro, here I thought you were planning on a challenge or some shit. I am fucking relieved, brother," the older man growled and rapped on the desk with his hands.

"What? No way, Hunter. You and Elissa, you are the only two who could possibly lead this Pride. I want a place here, and I assure you I am quite happy with my rank. Well, when I'm not distracted," he grumbled.

His cheeks burned with embarrassment as Hunter started asking him a whole slew of questions. It was pure fact that sex was natural, and some Shifters required a lot of it to steady the beast.

"When was the last time you *you know*?"

"Huh?"

"Oh, for fuck's sake. Sex, Pierce. I am asking when the last time was you had sex," Hunter growled, rubbing a hand over his ruddy face.

"Oh. Um. I don't know, a few months," he muttered, but Hunter just glared at him.

Fuck. Of course, the male could spot a lie. Duh.

"Fine. A Year."

"A year? You haven't had sex in a year?" the man gasped.

"Yeah. I haven't had sex in a year. So, what? I was

busy with school. It's not a big deal. Besides, I don't think my problem is sex, well, not just sex," he mumbled, a little embarrassed. "I am sorry I have been messing up. I swear, I will get my shit together."

A wide smile split Hunter's face, and the man nodded. Pierce felt relief wash through him. At least he wasn't getting kicked out. That was good. Of course, his situation hadn't changed. But yeah, he was still in the Pride.

"Don't worry about that, bro. We are gonna see you through this. So, your Tiger wants to settle down. How do you know?" he asked.

"Um, yeah. I mean, he's growly anxious, forlorn whenever we see mated couples. Fucker is keeping me up nights. I can't eat. I can't sleep. I can't focus for shit," he muttered.

"Okay. Yep. You need a mate, bro. So, have you called Uncle Uzzi?"

"Huh?"

Pierce's jaw dropped open. How the fuck had he completely forgotten about the pride's matchmaking guru? The man was practically on speed dial.

"Would that be okay? I mean, can I just email him or something?"

"Yes. Yes! Come on, you can do it right now,"

Hunter said, jumping up and allowing Pierce to sit in his chair.

The Tiger in him chuffed at the honor, but the human side of him was shitting bricks. Pierce sat down heavily, very much aware of the Neta watching him enthusiastically.

"Go on," he instructed.

Clicking the email app open, Pierce typed in Uzzi's name in the address line and the older Witch's contact info filled in.

Dear Uncle Uzzi,

He started the missive using the man's preferred moniker. He enjoyed being called uncle, and it was true he made everyone feel like family. *Okay, this was good,* Pierce decided and moved on.

It has been a while since you visited Maverick Point, and Hunter and Elissa both agree a visit is long overdue. I am hoping you can spare some time to come see us, well, me in particular. Or I can come to you. Whatever works.

Pierce paused, looking at Hunter for affirmation. The male nodded, and he continued. Going for broke, he decided on nothing but the truth. After all, engaging a matchmaker was no minor feat. He needed to start this with an open heart and mind.

You see, I am having some difficulties with my Tiger, and I need your help. I think the silly cat wants me to find a mate, but Uncle Uzzi, there is no one here who piques my interest.

I have been messing up at work, and Hunter is at his wit's end. He's forcing me to take some time off until I get my head on straight, but my Tiger is being surly as heck. Could I be right? Will a mate settle my inner beast?

So, I guess I am writing to ask you for your help. Is there anything you can do for me?

Thanks again.

Sincerely,

Pierce McDowd of The Maverick Pride

"Click send, Pierce," Hunter said when his finger hovered over the enter key.

He hesitated, wondering if this was the right call for the briefest of moments. Then, he went for broke, tapping the button with determined force.

"Sent."

Now, it was just a waiting game to see when the old Witch got back to him. If he got back to him.

Oh fuck, please get back to me.

Grrrr.

Chapter One

MAVERICK PRIDE

few days earlier...

Antonetta rolled her eyes at her computer screen. She'd been staring at the dang thing so long, the glare was giving her a migraine—unusual for a Shifter with supernaturally enhanced healing capabilities, but whatever.

She checked the time on the bottom right-hand corner of the screen. Ugh. It was almost nine o'clock at night, and she'd been in the office since dawn.

No life, Toni. You have no life.

Her ex's words played back in her head, but Toni shrugged them off. That turd had started texting her again this week, and it was fucking with her.

Are you really better off without me? Who else is going to want you?

Asshole. Yes, she was better off without him. As for who else would want her, how about nunya?

Nunya fucking business, turd breath, she growled the thought.

But Toni did not bother to reply. Stefan was in her rearview mirror, and that was exactly where she wanted him. They'd broken up a few months ago, but he still bothered her every couple of weeks.

His texts sometimes started out nice and sweet, and the first time he'd done it, she'd stupidly agreed to meet him for coffee. But that had turned out to be a terrible idea.

Not five minutes into their not-date, Stefan had started with the pressure on how she should accept his claim, and how she'd embarrassed him with his friends with her rejection. Then came the whole no one would ever want a cold fish like her as a mate, but he was willing to overlook her faults, etc.

Total fucking shit show. But still, it hurt. She was just glad she had met him in a public place filled with normals, so instead of causing a scene, he just watched her with anger glaring in his eyes as she dropped a ten-dollar bill on the table for the coffee she didn't drink and left.

After that, she blocked his number. Stefan was nothing if not determined, also known as stalkerish.

He texted from a different number a week later. And on it went. Now, she just blocked the new number he'd contacted her with and went on with her week.

Her phone buzzed, and she jumped, shaking the bad memories out of her head. She exhaled a relieved breath and swiped to answer the call.

"Toni, where the heck are you?" Adrianna, her sister, shouted through her cell phone.

"Sheesh. Indoor voices please. And I'm still at the office," Toni muttered, frowning at her damn computer screen.

"Are you serious?" her sister whined.

Toni blocked out the rest of what she was saying and read through the numbers again. She'd recently been given a promotion that involved moving to a completely different department within the Eat Well Live Proud corporation. It was an awesome opportunity for growth and a chance to move up in the company.

Granted, Toni had not had much experience with marketing, but she was creative, enthusiastic, and a hard worker. She'd taken many advertisement courses in school and online, and she was flattered the new head of marketing had asked for her by name.

A few months ago, Toni was given the chance to

run her own campaign. It was the opportunity of a lifetime. She'd been high on it for days, but when the excitement wore off, the hard work began. Her sisters had cheered her on, of course. The Goldens were a close knit group.

But this was the first time she was not working directly with them, and it had really challenged her skills and expertise. She'd been in charge of every-thing right down to the nitty gritty of what models to use, and where to spend on ads.

The campaign was launched a couple of weeks ago, and Toni was eager to see if it was getting results. EWLP had been her singular focus for so long, she was starting to wonder if maybe Stefan was right. Maybe she really had no life.

"Ade, I am sorry. I'll be there, I promise," she answered, but her sister was still going on and on.

Always so dramatic, that one. Sigh.

Maybe Toni was losing her mind. She mumbled to herself and re-checked the spreadsheets. Still, the numbers made no sense, and she was good with numbers. Mr. Bixby, her boss, had his own finance team running the money part of the campaign. But Toni liked to double check their work, and so far, it was not adding up.

Maybe she had the percents wrong, she

wondered. This marketing gig was a lot more pressure than she realized. But she supposed that was her fault. The Blue Valley Lion Pride owned and ran EWLP, and it was already a well-established firm.

Renowned as importers and exporters of the finest quality, organic, sustainably harvested, and eco-friendly meat and fish, their clientele included restaurants, hotels, and cruise ships. Just recently, they'd launched a line that delivered from farm/ranch/sea to table to customers the world over. That was the focus of Toni's marketing campaign.

EWLP Direct Line—delivering freshness direct to your door.

Catchy, right?

The new campaign ads featured couples and families from all walks of life cooking together, washing the produce, prepping the meals, and the reactions from the populace were amazing. Toni's ad was a success. She should be celebrating, going on vacation, something, but she couldn't stop. Not when the numbers were so wrong.

Even if they were right. Why would she stop? She had no mate, no cubs, not even a friend with benefits. She was a workaholic, and it showed.

"OMG! You are not even listening to me, ANTONETTA GOLDEN!" shouted Adrianna.

"Eeek. Sorry, sis," muttered Toni.

"Look, we're leaving for *Serious Moonlight* now. You better come or Mom is going to go apeshit," her sister scolded her through the phone.

Crap.

She'd forgotten the reason for tonight's shindig. The Golden girls were having a belated bachelorette party for their mother, who'd recently mated the King of the Blue Valley Pride.

Mom used to be such a cougar, but the little lady had settled down with Donovan Crowley. The Lion was the ruler of the Lions of Blue Valley. His first mate was Patricia's BFF, but love had blossomed between the two, and Toni had never seen her mother happier.

Of course, that did not stop the older female from partying like it was 1999.

Sigh.

"Just a few more minutes and I will be there," Toni mumbled, clicking the end call button while Adrianna was mid-tirade.

Her sister could be a little over the top. Besides, Toni was almost done. *Serious Moonlight* was a hopping place, and they used EWLP for everything now, so the food was excellent.

Her stomach grumbled, and Toni figured the least she could do was get a bite to eat. If she was lucky, her bro-in-law, Brock, would be on chef duty tonight. Lucky Ariella for snagging the talented Wolf.

Not that luck had anything to do with it. It was more like determination and mitigating circumstances. Now that they were mated, all the Goldens were regulars at the Dire Wolf owned establishment. Even baby brother George—*that finicky pussy.*

The youngest Golden was such a tight ass. Nothing at all like their free-spirited mother. Toni considered herself cautious, but George was downright boring. She wondered if he would be there tonight. Wouldn't matter either way.

Toni was only going for the food and to celebrate their mom. So what if the old broad got more action in one night than Toni had seen in years? She was fine being single.

Yup. It was great.

Liar, her Lioness hissed.

Who asked you? Besides, I have no time for romance.

Grrrr, was her she-Cat's only response.

Once bitten, twice shy, Toni was what you called

unlucky in love. She would meet her family tonight because she said she would, but she would go home alone. Safe, secure, and resigned to her solitude.

Sad Grrrrrrr.

Two hours later...

"You're late," Adrianna pointed out unhelpfully.

"I'm starving," Toni replied.

"Those guys are checking you out," her sister added, and Toni shrugged.

Men were always checking her out. It was not a big deal to Toni. She could hardly take credit for her face and curvy figure, that stuff was because of genetics. It was what happened when a man had to look past her warm amber eyes, thick dark tresses, and hourglass shape that kept her single.

"You gonna eat at the bar or get a table?" Adrianna asked.

"Bar is fine," she said, giving her order to Sheila, a redheaded fire brand who happened to be mated to the Pride's Prince.

"It'll be right out, Ton," Sheila said, sending the order straight to the kitchen using the new tablet system the bar had implemented.

The band was rocking, and Toni tapped her foot in time to the music. Adrianna had wandered off with some sweet talking male who'd asked her to dance, and Toni frowned. Her sister was a shameless flirt, but she never got serious with guys. She was even worse about dating than Toni.

"Hey, it's baby girl!" Patricia Golden-Crowley —*because her mother refused to give up her name completely, something Toni admired*—shouted as she grabbed Toni in a tight hug.

"Hi Ma," she replied, grinning automatically at the older female.

Unlike a typical bachelorette party, this little shin dig was going on after the mating and human marriage ceremony that took place immediately after. Not only that, but the King, i.e. the groom, was there as well.

"You are late, *sugar cub*. You know you work too hard," her mother shouted over the music.

"I know, Ma. Work. Sorry. Couldn't get away."

"That's okay, my lord and master was here to entertain," Patricia replied with a saucy wink at her mate.

The male was watching her with hooded eyes, love shining in them despite the din of the bar. Donovan Crowley was no fool. He was not going to sit home while Patricia got her groove on.

Smart man.

Toni's esteem for the Pride leader had gone up

immeasurably once she'd realized how much the male really loved her mother.

Where his new mate was concerned, the Lion proved wiser than any of the men her mother had dated after their father was out of the picture.

"You look happy, Ma," Toni said, smiling and leaning in as her mother grabbed her in a hug.

"I am happy, baby. And I want you to be too."

"Thanks, Ma," she replied, picking up her frosted mug and taking a pull of the cool, refreshing IPA.

Toni always appreciated whatever new flavors from local microbreweries *Serious Moonlight* had on their featured seasonal menu. This one had hints of orange and passionfruit that sang of summer sunshine and lazy afternoons. Not that Toni would know anything about that. Her days were full of work, and so were her nights, come to think of it.

Boy, was that depressing.

"You gonna dance, sugar cub?"

"Not now. Dinner first," she replied, grinning as Patricia danced away from her, stopping to wiggle her booty on the King who looked about two seconds from picking the female up, cave-Lion style, and carting her home.

Toni's imagination stopped there. She so did not want to know what the King and her mother got up to when they were alone. Having already had the unfortunate experience of walking in on the couple doing it wild style in her apartment, for fuck's sake.

So gross.

In truth, Toni still could not meet her new step-father's gaze even for a second. There was just so much she wished she could unsee.

Just ew.

She still got the heebie jeebies thinking about it. Still, they made a good couple. Speaking of the King, sitting at the bar with Donovan, was his son Leo, Sheila's mate, and some other Lion males from the Pride, including George.

Toni nodded at the bunch of males noncommittally. She searched the floor for her other sisters and saw Annabeth and Ariella shaking their tushes with their mates.

Crap, that meant Brock wasn't cooking.

Toni shrugged, knowing full well the male wouldn't leave his kitchen unless everything was running smoothly. She had high hopes for her Porterhouse steak with garlic smashed potatoes and sauteed broccolini and pity the sous chef who fucked that up.

There was one thing a person should never mess with, and that was a woman's dinner. The scintillating scent of perfectly cooked meat—rare, of course—and well-seasoned sides reached her nostrils, and Toni growled deep in her throat.

She was not worried about the normals, or humans, in the room. Their puny senses couldn't pick up her Lioness' elation at getting some good eats. She'd been depriving her inner beastie, working late hours, and living off take out. But this right here, this was the real deal.

"Here ya go," Sheila said, placing the plate down with a flourish.

"Thank you!" Toni enthused, taking a moment to let the flavors just saturate her olfactory senses.

Yowza. This was gonna be good.

"Oooh, steak. I want a bite!"

Toni's eyes flashed at her baby brother, who had stupidly reached over and grabbed her fork. Barely a second later, she had the idiot on his knees crying, his hand bent at an unusual angle as she ripped her fork from his slimy little clutches. Their little brawl was gaining some unwanted attention, but none of the other Lion males were about to step in.

Smart of them.

"Ah, I see sibling rivalry is alive and well," a slightly accented voice reached her ears above the music and the rest of the ruckus.

Toni turned her head to see one of her favorite people in the world taking the seat next to hers. She mushed her brother, pushing his oversized noggin out of the way and ignoring his gasp of pain, so she could greet the older Witch with a proper hug.

"Uncle Uzzi!" she shouted happily.

"Hello, my dear! You look marvelous," he told her, blue eyes twinkling. Uncle Uzzi looked her over, complimenting her, as any much loved honorary family member would.

"What are you doing here?" Toni said, sitting back down and cutting into her steak.

"I would not miss your mother's bachelorette party for the world! Now, tell me, how are you? Um, besides, starving, that is?"

Toni winked and took a bite, delighting in the wonderful flavors. She was not the type of woman to ever hide her appetite. Not in public. Not for anyone.

"I was working late," she explained, glad that she had some company now.

It was different, better, eating with a friend. The fact hit her suddenly that Toni was alone a lot. Eating by herself had become a habit quite by accident. Her late hours and the fact her sisters were finding mates left and right had left her by herself more than usual.

"I see. Too bad, isn't it?"

"What is?" she asked, chewing carefully.

Dang it, she was hungrier than she'd thought and was already halfway through her plate.

"It doesn't translate well, but it was something my liebling used to say to me whenever I worked late hours. She would tell me, Uzzi, you can take your work home, but you cannot take it to bed," Uncle Uzzi replied with a chuckle, his blue eyes sparkling. "It sounds better in German, I admit."

"I think it translates perfectly," Toni said, with a said smile. "It's not that I wouldn't like to eat with someone, Uncle Uzzi. But well, I was burned once. Truth is, I think my Lioness' mate meter is broken. She sure picked a doozy with that guy. But you know how that is."

"I see. So, your she-Cat wanted him, then?"

"Well, she wanted anyone, I think. She was so desperate for a mate, but I was all wrong for him, Uncle Uzzi. He wanted to move too fast, and I was reluctant, and then I started thinking, if I am hesitating maybe my Lioness is wrong. Maybe we aren't fated, and then she just shut down," she confessed quietly.

"That must be difficult, being at odds with your inner feline."

Uncle Uzzi sighed and offered her a small fire. The sparkle in his eyes dimmed a moment before flaring back up, and he tapped his chin.

"But you should not forget you are a Lioness, not a pussycat, Antonetta. Maybe it is time to give your feline another shot. Why not get back in the ring?"

"You mean why not try dating again?" she asked, surprised at how easy the solution came.

She shook her head, grabbed her beer, and took a long sip. The band moved on from hard rock to a slow ballad, and couples ambled slowly onto the floor. Toni watched them go. She sighed as one by one they started swaying and dancing, melting into one another.

Uncle Uzzi wasn't wrong. She did want that for herself. Her breakup with Stefan was a year ago and she'd been alone ever since. Her sisters had left it at that. They thought she was pining for her lost love, not knowing the details.

Only Adrianna knew the truth. She happened to catch Toni during one of her and Stefan's phone arguments. The male had been pressing her to accept his claim, and even though the lioness wanted him to be her fated mate, it did not feel right to her.

The argument had gotten ugly, and Toni was a wreck afterwards. Adrianna had helped her that night, blocking his number and changing the codes on her locks and all her passwords for safekeeping. She'd told Toni Stefan was a manipulator. Ade hated the guy, and Toni could not blame her.

If anyone made her sisters feel the way he had made her feel, Toni would kick the man's ass. So, she wised up. Even if Toni was to blame for their failure as a couple, she did not deserve his abuse.

She pondered the old Witch in front of her. He'd been matchmaking successfully for longer than she could count, and if he said it was time, it was possible it was. Maybe a year was long enough. Maybe it was time she tried again.

"Yes. Why not try dating?" he asked.

Shivers of fear raced up her spine and her stomach rolled at the thought of meeting another Stefan. Could she handle someone like that again? So smooth and sweet at first, then menacing at the end.

He'd highlighted all her faults, made her feel ugly and inadequate, and Toni did not like that at all. No. She just couldn't stomach that kind of thing. Not again.

"I don't think so, Uncle Uzzi," she told him. "I

mean, I have a great deal of respect for you and your reputation. But I'm just not cut out to be anyone's mate. I am married to my job."

She tried to laugh at the end, but the truth of it was actually kind of sad. The older Witch looked at her with sympathy radiating from his face. Toni swallowed a sob. She couldn't do this now. Not here. But Uncle Uzzi had a way with him, and the man patted her hand while she tried to get her emotions under control.

"Toni, I understand you have had disappointments in your past, but there is more to life than just work. If you allow me to look on your behalf, I think I can find what you need," he said quietly.

Antonetta looked around, Uncle Uzzi's hand still clasping hers, and she took in the whole bar scene. So many couples were there. Friends, relatives, people she knew from frequenting the place. They looked happy, especially those folks out there celebrating with her mother.

Did Toni really want to be alone for the rest of her life? The answer was a hard no. She wanted a mate, cubs, a family of her own someday.

Someday. Hmmpf.

That had always been her answer. But maybe someday was not good enough? Maybe someday was already here. She wasn't getting any younger. In her thirties, single, and with no prospects in sight.

Darn it, she sounded pathetic. She gnawed her lower lip before turning to Uncle Uzzi.

"Look, I can't make any promises right now, Uncle Uzzi. It's just I am incredibly busy with the new marketing campaign, and my numbers still aren't adding up," she confessed, huffing a sigh. "Ever since the company laid off Cornelia and her cronies, things have been weird at the office."

"I understand, dear. But what about you?" Uncle Uzzi asked before Annabeth and Hank ran over to the two of them.

"Toni, I didn't see you arrive," Annabeth said, giggling as her mate snuggled up behind her.

"Hey AB, how's little Toni doing?" she said to her sister, nodding at her little niece or nephew Annabeth was growing in her womb.

Toni was so happy for her sister, and she felt terrible for the pang of jealousy that hit her as she watched Hank nuzzle his mate's hair with pure adoration burning in his eyes. The formerly reluctant to be mated male was now the single most doting expectant father Toni had ever seen.

"How are you, Annabeth? And you, my boy?" Uzzi asked, grinning at the pair.

"Oh, we are great, Uncle Uzzi, but I have to drag this one home and tuck her in bed. She's about dead on her feet, but she'll never admit it," Hank said to the Witch, who was his honorary uncle.

The Falcon Shifter kept his hands firmly on his mate's protruding belly the entire time they chatted. After a few minutes, and one too many yawns from Annabeth, Hank swung her up in his arms, and left despite her protests.

What a love story that had been, she mused, watching after them. Toni had been with Annabeth during the whole *claim the cock*—cock as in bird, not phallus—hunt that went down. Her sister had well and truly fallen in love at first sight, both mating instinct and her heat kicking in to ensure the survival of their species had pushed her hard at the male.

Except Hank had other plans, and he'd tried to fight the pull of fate. It was a terrible time for her sister, which was why Toni felt completely unrepentant about the gift basket she'd helped organize once they were officially together.

The thing was ridiculous and complete with naughty X-rated toys, and her personal favorite—a gallon of sunflower seed butter with clear instructions for her sis to butter up her coochie "so the seagull gets to munching" written on neon notepaper.

Good times.

"Bye you two," Toni called out, laughing as Annabeth bit her mate's arm, to no avail.

The guy was relentless in the way he looked after her, and Toni thoroughly approved. Now that was good to see.

"I see that look on your face, Antonetta Golden, and I have only one thing to say. Don't you deserve to find that same kind of happiness?"

It was a good question. A really good question. Only problem was, Toni was not sure of the answer.

Did she deserve it?

Gulp.

Grrrrr.

The crowd at Serious Moonlight was happy, an air of celebration buzzed throughout. The music was upbeat and fun. Toni was surrounded by friends and family, and yet, sadness washed over her. She never felt as alone in her whole life as she did right then.

Sad grrrr.

Her Lioness growled and chuffed, and she rubbed the space over her heart. Poor kitty. Maybe she needed a little reconnect with her beastie. Yeah, probably she did.

So, she'd had a bad experience, a relationship gone sour. Didn't everyone have those in their rearview? People learned from mistakes, right? Learned and grew from them. Had she grown up? Maybe that was the real question.

Toni hated the self-doubt that plagued her. But when she turned back to look at Uncle Uzzi, still staring with that same question in his eyes, Toni knew she could not hide from the truth. Not anymore.

"You know something, Uncle Uzzi. I really don't know," she answered.

Grrrr.

Chapter Two

MAVERICK PRIDE

"Toni. Hellloooooo. Earth to Toni. Your phone has been beeping all morning," Adrianna grumbled in Toni's ear.

"What?" Toni jumped up from her slouched position on the sofa.

Dammit.

She fell asleep going over the new advertisements in the living room of the apartment she shared with her only remaining single sister. Shaking her head, she looked at the phone Ade was currently waving in front of her face.

"Dammit, Ade, stop," she grumbled and pulled on the thing.

"Eat my fur!" Adrianna replied snarkily and walked away.

Her sister refused to wear pajama bottoms, and she was currently sporting a crop top with the words *Farm Fresh Peaches* printed across it, and two images of the fruit right over her bazonkas. Beneath it she had on a pair of red granny panties, half of which had ridden up one cheek of her ample ass.

"Oh yeah? Well, pick your jam!" Toni called back, ignoring the middle finger Ade threw her way.

Beyotch.

Toni unlocked her phone, hard to do since she couldn't even see straight yet and frowned. There were like fifteen alerts from the legal department of *Eat Well Live Proud* and a furious email from her boss, Marion Bixby.

"Oh fuck," she moaned.

"What is it?" Ade said, returning with a cup of coffee so strong it was likely to put hair on her chest.

Undesirable side effect? Yes.

Necessary to function? Also, yes.

It sure wasn't easy being a woman in today's world. But that was not up for debate right then. Toni was re-reading each and every email to make sure she understood.

"My marketing campaign is being pulled," she said, disbelief filling her.

"What? Why? It looks so good," Ade questioned.

"They're saying I used copyrighted images illegally. I'm being sued! And not just me, the whole company!" Toni said, jumping up and dropping her mug.

"Toni!" Adrianna yelped as coffee spilled everywhere.

"Shit. I'm sorry, Ade, I have to go."

"Go, go. I got this," her sister said, concern written across her face.

Toni took the fastest shower ever, got herself dressed, and was in the office exactly thirty-seven minutes after reading her email. She'd been trying to locate the photographer she'd used for the ad shoot, but he was gone.

"I don't understand," she moaned aloud. "I did the research. I had him vetted. He came in here and we interviewed him together," she told Mr. Bixby, but the older male simply frowned.

"Ms. Golden, your work up till now has been exemplary, but EWLP cannot afford this sort of scandal in today's environment. I am afraid we have to let you go."

"You're firing me!" she gasped.

Toni had given everything to this job. It was all she had. What would she be without it? The room shrank. Its walls closing in on her, and Toni gasped.

She sat, *more like fell*, down hard into the empty chair in front of his desk.

"Not firing, no. You are on a leave of absence while our investigators and lawyers work on this matter. Please turn in your work laptop and refrain from moving anything work-related to your home computer. You must not interfere with the process, Ms. Golden. Thank you, you are dismissed."

Toni left the building, not even looking at her sisters, who watched her go from their cubicles. She was supposed to be the savvy one. The one who excelled at her job. The ice princess with no other life besides work.

Without work, what did Toni have?

It was a tough question, and it would require some thought…and tequila, she decided.

Lots of tequila.

L*ots of tequila later...*

.   .   .

"Oooh! Owie, owie," Toni moaned, rolling over from where she was splayed out on the floor in a perfect face-plant.

"There you are, sugar cub!" her mother screeched in a shrill voice.

"Mom?"

"Here you go," her mother said, so disgustingly pleasant it hurt Toni's ears.

Toni blinked and tried to sit up, missing twice before she got it right. What the hell happened last night? She recalled going to the palace, telling her mother she was basically fired.

She did not get into specifics, but her mom was ever the sympathetic one. She'd had the palace chefs prepare mountains of tacos and nachos, and she busted out the good tequila. Likely it had been spiked, Patricia Golden-Crowley was known as being partial to a little highly concentrated catnip.

Added to food or drink, that stuff could send the average Cat Shifter on a bender and a half. Toni and her sisters would know. Their mother, who was lovingly called Aunt Patty by most everyone who knew her, was a notorious prankster. But that was precisely why Toni had gone there. To help her forget the nightmare her life had become.

"Come on, kiddo, drink this," her mother said and handed Toni some godawful concoction.

Toni got a glimpse of whatever crazy gold caftan her mom was wearing, but it was too bright, so she closed her eyes again. Sounds of whimpering to the left and one good sniff told her Ade had joined the party at some point. As the only two single siblings left, it was only right they got wasted together.

I can't believe I might lose my job. Shit. Shit. Shit.

"What's in it?" Toni asked skeptically.

"No worries, my dear. It is not laced with anything by your mother. I made that brew for you specifically," a familiar voice said.

She blinked, wincing at the brightness of the room, and found the speaker almost instantly. Mortified at being discovered in such a state, Toni drank the thick liquid like a good girl. It was sluggish to swallow, bitter too.

"Ugh, this is terrible," she murmured and tried to finish it in one gulp.

"Medicine usually is my dear," Uncle Uzzi said gently.

Toni closed her eyes, willing herself not to puke whatever magic potion Uncle Uzzi had given her. In the background, she heard her mother and sister talking, well one was cajoling and the other was being a brat, but that was the norm for those two.

"Come on, Ade, you're next," Patricia said to her sister.

"No! Leave me alone," Adrianna retorted, her voice muffled by a pillow.

Toni just closed her eyes and exhaled. She stood up slowly, aware she was probably supposed to say something to the male Witch watching her as if she were a museum piece.

"Um, I am going to shower now."

"*Wunderbar!* I will be here when you get out. We have much to discuss, Antonetta Golden," Uncle Uzzi replied, his blue eyes sparkling with mischief.

"My life is so weird," she murmured, walking to the guest room she used whenever she stayed at the palace.

Toni had some clothes and toiletries stashed there for sister and mother sleepovers. Now that her mom was married to the King, they never had to worry about space again. Besides, she was tired of them trashing her apartment.

She felt sick. And not because of the exorbitant amounts of catnip laced tequila she'd imbibed last night. Was it even possible she'd been so grossly mistaken about the photographer?

Spike Jensen was highly recommended to her by Marguerite, another Lioness working in the marketing department at EWLP. Toni was new to that division, but she'd been with the company since her internship right out of high school.

She got her MBA before she was twenty-five. She worked in various departments, including sales with her sisters, before being given this opportunity. Just last week, Mr. Bixby had praised her for her marketing genius. Now she was being sued, could lose her job, and her professional reputation was in the literal crapper.

Everything was going great—*or so she'd thought. Damn. Damn. DAMN.*

Dressed and feeling a modicum better, Toni found Uncle Uzzi waiting for her in the small sitting room just outside the guest bedroom. The palace was known for its tasteful, though opulent décor, and this room was no different. High ceilings, thick carpets, lush furniture, classic paintings on the wall —it was, in a word, lovely.

"Come, my dear. Would you like some tea?" Uncle Uzzi said.

"Yes, please," Toni replied politely and joined him for a cup of the fragrant vanilla bourbon blend.

He poured, handing her the cup and saucer, and she fixed it with sugar and cream. After they were both settled, Toni started the ball rolling.

"Look, I know last time we chatted it might have seemed I was open to starting a relationship, but well, it's just not the right time," she said, stumbling over the words.

"Darling, it never seems like the right time. I understand your job is important, but is it safe to say you might be putting your eggs in one basket? A mate could help bear this burden with you," he told her gently.

"You know," she began, gearing up for what was doubtlessly going to be an uncomfortable confession. "Uncle Uzzi, I was almost mated once. That is, about a year ago, I was dating someone, and it got serious. He wanted to claim me, but I was reluctant."

She paused here. This part was hard for Toni. Ever the overachiever, knowing she was defunct in this particular thing, had her inner cat bristling, and her heart squeezing with pain and embarrassment.

"I see. Go on," Uncle Uzzi said, waiting for her to continue.

"I did not want to get mated. At least, not right

away. I was busy at work, and well, I wanted to wait to have a family. You know, being a Golden is not all that easy. My family has a reputation," she began, smiling tightly when Uncle Uzzi chuckled.

"My dear, your family is one of a kind. Truly, I have never met a group of female felines so supportive, so fun-loving, and so fiercely protective of one another. You Goldens are truly golden in my book," Uncle Uzzi said, shocking Toni to her core.

"Wow," she replied, placing her cup and saucer on the table. "I never heard anyone refer to us like that. Thank you, Uncle Uzzi."

"Why don't you tell me what this delusional male said to you, my dear?"

"Alright," she said, mustering her courage. "Stefan, my ex, said I was crazy to let him go because no one else would want me as a mate. He said my looks were the perfect trap."

"A trap?"

"Yeah, he told me men liked pretty faces and nice bodies, and mine were nothing more than an ad. But the reality would turn off all suitors besides him."

"I am not following, dear," Uzzi said, shaking his head. "What is the reality?"

"Well, according to Stefan, I'm a cold fish in bed," she said, hurrying through it. "He said my lack of sexual skills could be overlooked if I accepted his claim and started bearing him young," she told him tightly.

"What? Outrageous!" Uzzi growled. The older Witch's eyes blazed blue and little lighting sparks were buzzing along his fingertips. Toni raised her eyebrows and cleared her throat. She had never seen him so mad, wanting to ease his anger, she continued her story.

"Look, he's right. Our sex life was pretty bleh, and I am willing to take my share of the blame. I'm no Mata Hari. I mean, despite my family's rep, we don't sleep around, and honestly, after what he said, I have not taken another man to my bed—"

"In over a year, child?"

Toni shrugged uncomfortably. Yes, she missed sex. But who would want a repeat performance after being savaged by a lover?

"Living without sex is not really difficult," she lied, wincing when his expression changed to disbelief.

Of course, he could tell. Uncle Uzzi was not a Shifter, but he was magical.

"Sorry. I am just not used to talking about my sex life out loud," she apologized.

"I understand. But you should know, I have been

doing this job for a very long time. I have seen your face when you see your sisters with their mates. You can't tell this old man you don't want that, too. Tell me what's stopping you. Maybe you will feel better after you unload it all," he told her gently.

Toni exhaled. Could it be that simple? Maybe he was right. Either way, Toni was no coward. She was a Lioness. Not a kitten.

"Look, I have toys and romance novels to keep my needs met," she began. "But maybe that's why I'm no good at real sex. Maybe romance novels have gotten my expectations too high."

Toni shrugged. It was a plausible notion. The men in novels were simply unattainable in real life. Then again, maybe she was just too high mainte-nance for real men.

"Darling, I do not believe that for a second. Sex is not a singular sport. Sexual partners each have a responsibility, and really it should be more than that, it should be a desire, a need even, to see to the other's needs. If one partner is not wholly involved, then the other partner should speak up, ask ques-tions, find what works."

"Ideally—"

"Not ideally, actually. Look, Toni, I am not sure what made you date a man like that, but if that scoundrel had to put you down and deliver ultimatums, he was just not the man for you. Relationships are complicated, no doubt, but they should be based on mutual respect and caring, not on unrealistic demands and criticisms," Uncle Uzzi said with conviction.

Toni exhaled slowly. He was right. Of course he was. Relationships were based on respect and caring, at least the good ones were. Stefan was never really interested in her as a person, only in what she could bring him in terms of bragging rights and offspring. The old Witch truly was a wonder.

"It feels good to hear that, Uncle Uzzi. Thank you," Toni admitted. "Um, my ex really shook my confidence. I've been gun shy ever since."

"Of course you have, You are a woman who feels things deeply, and I imagine he cut you very badly. I am sorry for it, but hiding out won't help, you know? You might not want to hear this, but I think you let this person have too much control over you, Toni. It is time to let him go," Uncle Uzzi stated strongly.

She could have cried at how simple the solution was. Blocking the man's number and deleting his texts did nothing to stop his hold on her. He was still fucking with her life, and Toni had had enough.

"You're right. You are absolutely right. I am beginning to think I let Stefan mess with my head because it was easier than trying to work through our differences or admit that I was wrong about him," she confessed.

For the first time since they broke up, Toni did not feel guilty about it. The past year, she had been beating herself to death every time she thought about her ex. Thoughts like what was wrong with her, and the feeling she was not good enough, had haunted her. But just saying out loud that maybe he was not the man for her sort of clicked everything into place.

Toni felt relieved.

"Uncle Uzzi, thank you. I think that did help."

"Good. Now, about finding you a match, my dear," he continued. "I think if you allow yourself the right to be happy, you will find it, and if you are open to the opportunity, you might find the person the Fates have picked out just for you."

"Well, wait a second. I mean, I was too busy to ask for your help before and now my integrity is being questioned at work. I could even be sued! The timing just sucks. I think you have definitely helped me see Stefan and I were just wrong together, but even that is still new," she said.

"Sometimes we need someone to help us through the healing process, Toni."

"But, Uncle Uzzi, what kind of mate would I make right now with all of these problems?"

"My dear, you would be surprised. Will you hear me out?"

"I suppose so."

"Good, now how do you feel about weekend getaways?"

"Like a vacation?"

"Precisely! I know the prettiest little woodland area with cabins for recreational use. It is completely Shifter friendly. You could give your Lioness space to roam, hunt, even swim."

"I mean, that sounds great."

Toni shrugged, listening as Uzzi continued to list the pros of a mini vacation in wonderful detail.

It couldn't really hurt, could it? Going away to meet a strange man might be fun. It was definitely romance novel worthy, and Toni was an expert with thousands of titles read and even more loaded onto her eReader.

At the very least, she could forget about work for a little while. And what was the worst that could happen, a bad date? She'd had those already.

One little dinner, then she could spend the rest of

her time on a relaxed impromptu vacay reading and letting her Lioness roam the forest. It sounded like a dream.

"Uncle Uzzi, I am in!"

What did she have to lose?

Chapter Three

P ierce hopped inside his suped up Wrangler. The top was on, and the windows rolled up since it was about to thunderstorm.

Crazy ass weather.

He whistled and drummed his fingers on the steering wheel as he turned down the dirt road. The Maverick Pride House was located near some prime New Jersey forestland. As such, the Neta had a few cabins built up in the woods to be used by Pride members for getaways and such.

It was private land, secluded for the safety of their kind. A Tiger could just cut loose and roam. But that was not why Pierce was headed to the cabins.

Exactly one day after he sent an email to the

magical matchmaking guru, Uzzi Stregovich, the older Witch replied with a list of explicit instructions. First, he had to fill out a form which was basically a mate wish list.

He'd felt silly doing it, but Pierce's beast was so riled lately, he had no choice. Dutifully, he sat down in his Neta's office with the male himself. Hunter insisted on being part of the whole process for whatever reason, Pierce had no clue. But he did as he was told and answered every single one of the Witch's questions as honestly as he could.

He wanted a woman who was sweet, docile, supportive, cheerful—a real nurturer. Yeah, that sounded good.

The drive was not too bad, just forty-five minutes up the mountain. It was late June and unseasonably cold. They'd had tons of rain the past few weeks, and he was hoping for a bit of sunshine.

Turning into the graveled driveway for cabin 135, Pierce slowed to a roll, finally stopping the Jeep as he watched a drop dead gorgeous female playing tug of war with an enormous, wild black bear.

"Holy fucking shit," Pierce mumbled, jumping out of the Jeep. "Lady, I don't know who you are, but you need to drop that bag and back away from the bear."

His heart was pounding so hard, the Tiger inside of him roaring loudly, Pierce could barely think. Was she some kind of nut job?

"What? Who the heck are you?" the female asked.

"Just drop the bag and back up slowly," he repeated the instructions, stepping cautiously forward.

The bear's growl deepened, the animal aware of his presence. His inner Tiger was on high alert. The bear grunted, his maw closed tight over what appeared to be a reusable burlap bag full of groceries. The beast had to be over six hundred pounds, and sure, he smelled fur on the female, but if pushed came to shove, she could be hurt.

The time it took for her to shift into whatever she was would be too long. Precious seconds counted in any battle, especially one with an animal like that. The strange female would not come out of that scuffle unmarked. Pierce was not having any of that. Not on his watch.

"No way. Look, beat it, pal. I got this," the spunky female grunted, dismissing Pierce without even a look.

Damn. She was hot. A bit unhinged, but cute as a button. She had long, shapely legs and a firm, round bottom outlined in tight black jeans. It would be a damn shame if a single inch of the beauty met with the bear's wickedly sharp claws.

Pierce moved closer, trying to get in front of her. But the bear had other plans. Big bastard tugged her a few feet away from him, dragging her closer to the tree line.

Shit. That was not good. The woman snarled at the beast and pulled on the surprisingly strong strap with all her might. It was a lot of might too, Pierce realized, duly impressed.

"Dammit, Yogi, I said let go," she told the bear, who did not seem fazed.

Her sandaled feet skidded across the lot as the growling bear pulled back. Shit. This was going to get ugly.

"You named him?" Pierce asked, scoffing at the woman's complete lack of awareness that the wild animal could kill her so much as look at her.

"These are my cookies, you dumb bear! Let go!" she shrieked, and the bear growled louder.

Fuck.

Pierce was already pulling off his clothes, his Tiger clawing to get out of him. The female shrieked, landing on her ass as the bear gave one hard pull. The monster of an animal stood on his hind legs, the burlap strap still hanging from his maw as he opened his mouth and roared.

Pierce's transformation was fast, and before the bear could attack, he'd already leaped over the woman. His Tiger was a big bastard, and he roared right in the bear's face. Wild animals usually recognized there was something different about Shifters.

The animal snorted, falling back on all fours. He pawed the ground, backing up a step, then two. Pierce's Tiger stepped forward, herding the monster away from the woman. The bear did not want to retreat, his tiger could tell, and that made his animal even madder. He roared again.

Mine. Back the fuck off or I'm gonna turn you into a throw rug, he thought angry beyond reason.

The bear gave one last shake of his big, boxy head before turning around and taking off, the grocery bag still clenched between his jaws. Pierce followed the creature with his Tiger's sharp gaze until he could no longer make him out in the dense forest before turning back to stare at the woman.

"Oh, that is just great," she snapped, getting up off the floor and wiping gravel from her sweet as a peach ass. "Now, what did you do that for? That bag had my double stuffed cookies in it. Ugh. Man!

Damn you, Yogi!" she shouted at the woods, tiny fist raised.

Her pouty mouth turned down in an angry scowl as she cursed the poor bear out, and that right there was when Pierce lost his heart. He shifted back to his skin, panting a little at the rapid change back and forth. But even the uncomfortable tingle from the aftermath of his shift could not stop a grin from cracking across his face.

Damn, she was feisty and cute as hell. Finally, she looked at him, and he was stunned by clear, amber eyes like hot maple syrup.

Holy shit.

Pierce's heart stopped. Did he say she was cute? The female was a fucking knockout. Those stunning eyes dropped down to his cock, and all the air seemed to leave his lungs. He couldn't help it if he was hard as stone.

"You have a boner," she stated, her gaze flicking back to his.

"I do," Pierce replied.

No point in lying. She had eyes. Besides, she was a Shifter—*sniff,* make that a Lioness.

The sexy as hell female could scent a lie as easily as he could. Frozen to the spot, Pierce did not move a muscle. And no, he did not cover himself right away, either. She seemed to like looking, and if he was being honest, he liked that she liked looking.

Grrrr. Mine.

His heart had started up again. The damn thing was beating inside his chest so hard, he was sure she could hear it. Slowly, he bent down and grabbed his discarded jeans.

"Um, I'm Toni, uh, Antonetta Golden, Blue Valley Pride. Um, people call me Toni," she mumbled.

Clearing her throat before she turned around, Pierce had a second to admire her pert backside before he got dressed. He tugged his pants on, one leg at a time. His Tiger was tearing him up on the inside, the animal wanted to get closer to the woman.

Fast as a lightning strike, Pierce McDowd had his mind made up. This woman was his. Or she would be. Soon.

"Nice to meet you. Pierce McDowd, Maverick Pride," he replied, turning to face her with his hand outstretched.

Toni stared at it for a beat longer than normal. Finally, she took it, sending shockwaves of aware-ness zipping through his veins. He noticed the stiff-ening of her back, and he smiled. Good. She felt it, too.

"Um, did Uncle Uzzi send you?" she asked shyly.

"Yes, he did. And I am really, really glad," he replied, easily.

Truth. Truth. SO MUCH TRUTH.

Bells were going off in his brain, but not the warning kind. These were more the *ring-a-ding-a-ding-we-got-a-winner-here* kind of bells. He cleared his throat, tracing every inch of her with his eyes and committing it to memory.

"Oh, well, I just got here. I brought some snacks, well, I had some snacks, but the bear got it," she mumbled, hands in her back pockets.

The stance caused her chest to thrust out nicely, and he had to swallow a growl. Lord, the woman was stacked. Usually, Pierce got to know someone before he wanted to jump their bones. Not with Toni, though.

The female triggered something primal inside him. Heat and arousal permeated the air, Toni's mouth opened, interrupted by the sudden grumble of her belly. She blushed, but shrugged it off and damn, that was sexy, too. Both beast and man wanted to stake a claim. Now. Right now.

Mine.

"Are you hungry?" he asked, concerned.

"Oh, I'm a Lioness. I'm always hungry," she replied without guile.

"Me too," he added, smiling even wider than before.

Cute and honest. This was going to be fun. Pierce was glad she had confidence and didn't bother with those silly little games other females had tried on him. Toni didn't try to hide the fact her stomach had growled, she just owned that shit.

As she should. Beautiful bear wrestling badass.

Shifters were big eaters in general, and he hated having to hide the fact he could eat. Even so, he'd dated plenty of female Shifters who liked to pretend they were satisfied with half a burger or a small salad.

Fuck that.

He'd always preferred a woman who was comfortable in her own skin, and Toni showed no signs of being anything but. Thank fuck. Pierce wouldn't have to waste time trying to convince her she was beautiful. The woman simply was and seemed aware of it without conceit.

Damn, that was hot. But confidence was always sexy. Well, to him it was. Some guys liked to keep their women guessing whether they were attracted to them. Not Pierce. He wore his heart and his appreciation right there on his sleeve.

Hell, right then, he was sure it was written all over him. He had it bad. His desire for the female was likely glowing like a neon sign scrawled right across his forehead.

"Um, why don't we see what's inside the kitchen? Uncle Uzzi said it would be stocked."

"Okay. Let's do that, pretty girl," he said, the pet name just rolled off his tongue.

He froze to see if she would chew him out over it, but she simply paused. Her warm amber eyes met his, and he cocked his head, noting the crimson hints of a blush spreading up her neck and across her cheeks.

She was even prettier when she blushed. The woman was clearly not used to compliments. Pierce was downright shocked, but it showed. Even her scent had turned slightly tart with embarrassment, and he frowned thoughtfully.

How could a woman who looked like that be bashful about compliments?

Oh, she was doing it now, piquing his interest with more than just her face and heavenly body. Pierce didn't know what kind of fuckheads she hung around with, but clearly, they were all imbeciles.

"Alright then," she mumbled and turned around.

He followed her lead up the stairs, already making a mental note to compliment the shit out of her. Pierce's Tiger rumbled inside him. Even the beast liked the idea of flattering her to get more of those sweet, pink blushes. Of course, he would mean every word.

But yeah, he could make a habit of telling her nice things. Hell, he could make it the new normal.

Fuck yeah, that sounded good.

Chapter Four

MAVERICK PRIDE

"Oh my fur, you ate four frozen supreme pizzas!" Toni declared, shocked and somewhat impressed.

Pierce raised one eyebrow, swiping a chip from the basket that sat between them. The man didn't even look full yet. Heck, he was still rummaging around for something else to sink his mighty sharp teeth into.

"You ate two," he pointed out unhelpfully.

"Rude," Toni replied. "You aren't supposed to comment on how much a lady eats."

"Why? I think you look sexy when you eat," he said, propping his forearms on the table and leaning over.

No elbows. Nice.

"Sure I do." Toni gave an unladylike snort.

"I speak the truth," Pierce said. "You chew more than any Shifter I have ever seen. It's cute and lady-like. Also, I like you're honest about food. I hate when people pretend to live on spinach leaves and water. I don't. I mean, I'm a Tiger, I eat all the time. Nice to sit and eat a meal with a woman who is comfortable with her love of pizza," he said, a hint of teasing in his voice at the end.

That was new, Toni thought. Lion males ate like pigs, but many of the Lionesses she grew up with acted like that. Not her sisters, of course, but she remembered sleepovers or parties before school dances where the girls all ate before the guys arrived because they didn't want them to think they were heifers. It was all weird to Toni, and she never did play into it. Even so, it was nice to hear him speak honestly.

Okay, he likes that I eat.

She'd heard the truth in his voice, but the way he dropped compliments left and right was enough to make her head spin. Maybe that was the point. He sure was handsome, sexy as sin truthfully, and Toni wondered what he needed a matchmaker for.

"What are you thinking about?" he asked.

"I was wondering why you contacted Uncle Uzzi," she said, going for broke.

"We can have that talk any time you want, Toni, but the truth is, I don't think you're ready yet. How about we ease into it?" he asked.

"Alright. Easy does it," she replied.

Pierce nodded, his aqua gaze glued to hers, and she shivered involuntarily. The gleam in his eyes made certain long forgotten parts of her stand up and take notice. She'd never seen such eyes on a person before, and they were positively mesmerizing. Not quite blue or green, but some mystical combination that seemed to inspire passion and evoke curiosity.

"Okay, so what are we supposed to do? Just like, share the cabin for the weekend?" she asked, determined to quit staring.

This was ridiculous. She was a grown ass Lioness. Not some cub who'd never spent the night with a boy. But this was new, she had to admit. Her body was reacting to his nearness in ways she would have never expected.

Didn't matter. They weren't sleeping together the first night. Or maybe not ever. Her Lioness took exception to that. The big Cat had been watching

Pierce with unwavering attention ever since she'd seen him leap over her to chase that bear away.

Grrrrr.

"Yeah. I mean, it's a vacation," he said, interrupting her train of thought.

"Vacation?"

"Yep. So, what do you normally do on vacation?" he asked.

"I don't know. I don't normally go on vacation," she admitted.

"Ah, workaholic?" he asked, and he was teasing, but it still made her nervous.

"Yeah, actually," she said, gauging his reaction. "I think it's important we start out truthfully with each other, if slowly. See, for a while now, work was the most important thing in my life."

"But it's not now? How come?"

"Are you fishing for information, Pierce McDowd?" she replied with a question.

Truth was, Toni really hoped he was fishing for more info on her. It was not every day a man who looked like him stuck around to chat Toni up.

Her rep as an ice queen meant the only guys brave enough to approach her were narcissists or ego maniacs. But not him. Oh no, Pierce McDowd was something else.

Sexy, tempting boy with soul-piercing eyes.

"I want to learn everything I can about you, but I'm a patient man, Miss Golden," he said, a grin playing at the corner of his sexy mouth. "Tell you what. We can go for a hike after we clean up."

"That's a good idea. Maybe we can shift," she said, and her thoughts returned to images of Pierce just after his earlier change to his beast.

The Tiger was gorgeous, and the man even more so. Toni would not mind getting another peek. Of course, the moment Toni agreed thunder boomed and lightning flashed outside the huge ceiling to floor glass windows that made up the one entire side of the cabin.

Mother Nature sure was a pussy-blocking beyotch sometimes.

"I guess not," he replied with a bark of laughter.

They made quick work of the kitchen, clearing their junk food feast and playing twenty questions. It was the kind of thing she hadn't done since she was a kid, and never with a boy she was interested in— and she was interested.

She could admit that, even if only to herself. Anything else would be a boldfaced lie. Pierce McDowd was interesting AF.

"Lemme get this straight, you dunk pizza crust in diet cola?"

"Yup. Cheese puffs too," she told him, grinning when he made a face of abject horror.

"Toni, that mouth of yours has had me hypnotized since the moment I saw you, but your questionable snacks leave me wondering if maybe I was dropped on my head as a cub," he teased.

"Hypnotized, huh? That's a good one," she said, turning around to watch the rain pelting the glass.

It was shockingly beautiful. The power of the sudden storm beating against the glass. Lightning struck very close by, and she jumped, eyes wide at the trees shaking in the fierce wind and the absolute raw beauty of it.

"Easy, pretty girl. This window wall is made using top of the line insulated glass panels. No lightning is coming through them."

"It's really something else. Did you, uh, did you build this?"

"Maverick Development built all the cabins here. This is Pride land."

"Oh, I see, and you work construction?" she asked, and looking him over, well, it was obvious.

The Tiger Shifter was massive. He had wide shoulders with thick cords of muscle circling his arms and chest, down his belly and legs. He wasn't gym rat buff, but he was big, and he was strong. She could just tell.

"I worked for Maverick Development since I was eighteen," he said, a little evasively, but it was the truth. "See here, we used towering pine trunks from the woods here to frame the glass. The perfect merger of nature and tech."

"It looks amazing," she agreed.

The tree trunk frame and seamless glass made it look as though she were standing in the forest the deeper she stepped into the room. The entire first floor of the cabin was an open design with no walls separating the rooms. The kitchen, dining room, and living room all flowed together, with access to an outside terrace. Even in the middle of the storm, it was breathtaking.

"How about a movie?" he asked, turning to the huge entertainment system on the opposite side of the room.

"Sure. What are our options?"

Pierce ran down a list, and after a little while they decided on a horror spoof flick they'd both seen a million times but could always watch again. She had never had so much fun.

"I'll make popcorn," she told him, turning to go

back to the kitchen.

It didn't matter that they'd just eaten enough to choke a pig. She could always use a snack. The cabin's kitchen was equipped with an air popper, and microwave oven, and a dozen other gadgets and gizmos. It was like glamping, she mused, wondering what her sisters would say if they could see her now.

"You put salt on this?"

"Yep. And butter," she said, grabbing a handful before taking a pull from her bottle of beer.

She brought one for him too, settling down next to him on the enormous love seat.

"I can't believe I am sitting here with a virtual stranger watching a scary movie in a cabin in the woods. It's like a scene from this movie," she scoffed, laughing when he made choking sounds.

"You think I'm some kind of serial murderer?"

"Well, I don't know you," she teased, shrugging her shoulders.

"Yes, you do. I'm Pierce, remember? Handsome Tiger, saved you from a wild bear—"

"I did not need saving," she interrupted, but he just went on like she had not said anything at all.

"Besides, pretty girl, I saw you text my picture to someone, likely asking for the lowdown. Was it Uncle Uzzi?"

"When did you see that?"

"When you thought I wasn't looking, but I am glad you did, Toni Golden. Shows you're smarter than the average kitten."

Oh snap. He caught that, did he?

"See, now I am thinking maybe this whole thing is not a good idea. I mean, yes, I did take your picture to get confirmation of your person. I mean, you don't just meet some hot guy in the woods and decide, yay, vacation buddies. Besides, you took off your clothes seconds after meeting me and tried to wrestle a bear. Clearly, you have *knight-in-shining-armor* issues. And another thing, I am no kitten," she stated.

"Okay," he said, nodding and placing his beer bottle on the coffee table before hitting pause on the movie.

"First, I said I approved of you finding out who I was for sure by texting Uncle Uzzi, but I apologize if that came off as condescending. I did not mean it that way at all. I am well aware you are a badass Lioness, and again apologies if you don't like being called kitten, I meant it more like sexy little kitten, and not cub, but I get it if you don't like that pet name," he said, pausing a second before starting up again.

"Also, might I remind you, you were actually wrestling a huge black bear by yourself before I arrived with my *knight-in-shining-armor* issues. Don't get me wrong, I think you are a total badass. Hear that? You. Are. A. Total. Badass. I don't pretend for a minute you needed me to rescue you from that bear, but I really could not help myself. Tiger wasn't having any chance of you being hurt," he whispered the last bit, having emphasized the badass part in a crisp, even voice that gave her shivers.

Shivers. Shivers. SHIVERS.

"Last, and perhaps the strongest argument as to why this," he continued, gesturing between them, "is a fantastic idea, Antonetta Golden, is that *you* think *I* am hot."

"Ha!" she gasped her laughter.

Damn the man for being a good listener! She was grinning like crazy at him, and the Cheshire-worthy smile that split across his ridiculously hot face.

"Okay. Okay. So, really? That is how you're going to close? *I* think *you're* hot."

"that's my story and I am sticking to it," he teased some more. "You aren't denying you stated that, are you? There are witnesses."

"Witnesses?"

"Yeah. me. Anyway, that was not a question. So,

are we ready to move onto the hard ones?" he asked, taking a sip of beer.

"The hard ones. What are the hard ones?" she asked dumbly.

Toni was having some trouble concentrating, but who the heck could blame her? The lights were dim. Her heart was pounding. The storm having created a sort of charged atmosphere had her skin buzzing and her Lioness hyperaware of every move the man made.

"You wanted to know why I contacted Uncle Uzzi, right?"

"Um, yeah. I did."

"Well, that's an easy question to answer, Toni Golden," he murmured.

He was so close she could smell the strawberry licorice rope he'd just eaten on his lips. Anticipation hummed in the air, alive and zipping between them. She wanted his kiss.

Craved it, even. And just when she thought he was going to give in, Pierce leaned down, bypassing her lips to whisper in her ear. His fingers sent shivers down her spine as they brushed across the sensitive skin there, tucking her hair back.

Ooh, she could smell him now. Gods, he really was hot. Face like a movie star, body like an

Olympian, and smelling like forest and fur, man and musk, Toni was falling under his spell and fast. Anticipation had the butterflies in her stomach turning into fighter jets as Pierce's lips grazed her earlobe.

"A Shifter contacts Uncle Uzzi for one reason, right?" he asked.

Toni nodded her head, leaning in closer to his warmth. She closed her eyes, every fiber of being tense with the need to hear his answer.

"I contacted him because I wanted him to find my mate," he told her, his gravely voice doing delicious things to her insides. "I wanted him to find *you.*"

Oh fuuuuuuucccckkk. That did it.

Any hope she'd had of resisting the sexy as sin male was gone after that. It had been a really long time since Toni had felt a connection to someone, and never was it like this. With no thought for her own sanity or self-preservation, she went in for the kill.

Wrapping her hands around his neck, Toni tugged Pierce to her for a kiss that was as charged as the storm raging outside. All the while, her inner Lioness growled one word.

Mine.

Chapter Five

oly. Shit.

Pierce froze for one long moment after Toni pulled him down and smashed her sweet lips against his. Her eyes glittered intensely, like the predator she was when she came at him, but he could handle her.

One. Single. Moment.

That was all he allowed himself to catch up to what was happening. Was this sexy as sin, smart as a whip, funny little Lioness making the first move with him? Fuck yes, she was. And wasn't that hot?

During that frozen moment in time, Pierce was immovable. Frozen. Rooted to the spot. Hell, he might as well have been a statue—*then she sighed.*

Shivers raced up his spine, and it was like the

entire world just clicked into place. It was a sweet, soft expulsion of sound. So small, it was barely a whisper, but it might have been a roar for the effect it had on him. Blood pumping, heart pounding, his beast growling a chorus inside of him, only it comprised one word and one word only—*mine*.

Suddenly, Pierce was alive again. Alive and moving. He used one hand to cradle the back of her head, pressing her closer to him as his tongue begged entry to her mouth. Toni turned, pressing her heavenly body flush against his, and that naughty little sigh sounded once more, then Pierce was in. Home free and taking everything she was giving, offering her himself in return.

He growled roughly, unable to keep his tiger at bay. The monster in him wanted her, too, and Pierce allowed it. He deepened the kiss, losing himself to this surprising woman, this peach flavored passionflower.

Who the fuck had called her cold? She was a goddamned inferno in his arms. Fuck that guy. He had no place here. No one did besides the two of them. And that was just the truth, wasn't it? If it was only ever Pierce and Toni, all would be right with his world.

He imagined Toni hadn't been kissed like this in a very long time, if ever. That satisfied something primal inside him. He wanted it to be good for her, special, like it was for him. Coils of pleasure unfurled inside of him, and Pierce realized he was getting addicted.

That was dangerous. She was dangerous. But he'd never shied away from that sort of thing before. After his email, Uncle Uzzi had called him to conduct a little interview, and the male Witch had said something that stuck with Pierce. He'd asked him if Pierce was ready for the changes finding his mate would bring.

Pierce had said yes, but he didn't know it would be like this. He couldn't know. Hell, he felt as if he'd been born again. Like his life had taken on a new meaning and it revolved around Toni. Like she was his sun and his moon.

She was special. He felt that intensely. Special and kissing him with abandon, covering him with her delicious scent. Pierce angled his head, growling as he sipped from her lips and the woman just melted into him.

Her submission humbled him. She was a powerful Lioness, but she didn't try to best him. Toni was gifting him with this softness she likely didn't give to anyone else, and Pierce wanted to roar it to the world.

Mine. Mine. Mine.

Some deep, dark, utterly caveman-like part of him grunted in satisfaction at that thought. She was his and yes, that made him possessive, territorial, all those terrible alphahole qualities he always swore he'd never feel.

But even more than the terrifying need to mark her with his bite, Pierce was filled with the desire to make her feel good. To make sure she knew she was cared for, coveted, safe.

Shit. This is big. Life-changing.

When was the last time he felt protective of a female? Easy answer. Never. Pierce rarely dated, and when he did, it was never serious. The women were typically Shifters. They understood he had needs, and they had their own. It was all mutually consensual fun. Nothing heavy.

But with Toni, this felt heavy. Like fucking huge.

He plucked at her lips, lapping tenderly at her sweet mouth. Every single nerve ending in his body was abuzz with desire and awareness. Her plump lips were the perfect landing zone for his kisses, and her tongue, fuck, her tongue was goddamn magic.

Ever the Hunter, he chased after it with his own, loving the way she tangled with him.

Heaven.

Kissing her was like pure heaven. Like he'd been waiting his whole life for her, and Pierce felt that right down to his marrow. His body ached. No, it was more than that. It burned for her. Like he'd been asleep forever and was finally waking up.

He'd never felt so turned on from just kissing. Christ, the woman was so fucking good at this. She was knocking him out, driving him crazy, and capturing his heart without even trying.

Sweet, sexy, pretty, pretty girl. Fierce, badass, funny woman. Mine.

Yes, he wanted so much more than to kiss her. But he wouldn't rush this. He couldn't even if he tried. The Tiger would not allow it.

Time lost all meaning as they kissed, and kissed, and kissed on that couch. The world ceased to exist, and Toni was the only thing that mattered. Her hands moved to his shoulders, those tiny digits clinging to him, and yes, he loved it.

She felt so good in his arms, molded to him from hip to mouth. The curve of her breasts felt so damn good against his chest. Their pebbled tips bit into his flesh through the layers of fabric.

Pierce never thought of himself as shallow. He was not moved by beauty alone. But Toni had it all. Holy hell, the woman was a veritable bombshell with her pin-up girl figure, her cover model face, and her wicked sharp mind. Oh, she had layers, and had been gifting him with teasing glimpses of them all day until he was utterly besotted.

He was greedy, though. He wanted more. He wanted it all. But he knew better than to rush. Secrets had to be earned, and Pierce made up his mind then to be the man to earn hers.

"Mmm," she moaned softly.

It was that sweet, soft vulnerability that did him in. Her eyes were closed, and she looked so damn pretty. It was going to kill him, but he knew what he had to do.

Reining in his monster Cat, Pierce slowed the kiss until his lips were barely brushing against hers. It felt so good, the whisper light touches, he could have continued doing that for who knows how long. Just sliding his lips against hers, breathing her air, worshipping her with his mouth.

Toni sighed, and he shivered, rubbing his nose along hers, his cheek next. It was a sign of affection all felines recognized. It was also a way to transfer his scent to her. A fact his inner beast reveled in.

Possessive much? Hell. Yes. Unapologetically so.

He pressed his cheek against hers one last time and lifted his face, cupping her cheeks gently. When she lifted her heavy lids and those golden amber beauties flashed at him, he saw curiosity, but not anger.

Thank fuck.

"Should, uh, should I press play?" he asked.

"Um, yeah, sure," she whispered, her posture stiffening.

The last thing he wanted her to feel was rejection, so Pierce decided to nip that in the bud right then. He held her hand, stopping her from sliding away. Not quite ready for that sort of distance. Not yet, maybe not ever.

"This isn't me saying no, Toni," he murmured.

"It's not? Because you were the one who stopped," she replied, not looking at him.

Oh no. He wasn't having that. Pierce touched her chin with his forefinger, gently cajoling her to turn his way. When she did, he kept his gaze steady on hers.

Easy does it. Just tell the truth.

"You don't get it, do you, pretty girl?" he asked, cocking his head as he took her in.

She was so pretty, and the thing about it was, she

was not conceited at all. If ever a woman should be, it was her. Pierce had met plenty of females who thought they were all that, and they demanded the attention they believed was their due. But not her.

Here Toni was, still glowing from their kiss, her lips all plump and glistening, and her cheeks blushing a pretty pink, but it was like she had no idea the picture she made. Fucking gorgeous. The woman was a heartbreaker, and she had him already. He was a fucking goner.

Hook. Line. Sinker. I am hers.

"Toni, I want more than to fool around on the couch with you."

"I get it, I was never very good at this anyway," she murmured, blushing crimson.

"Are you serious? Woman, you really don't get it," he growled, grabbing her hand, and pressing against the hard evidence of his arousal.

"Oh! Then why?" she asked, her hand still on his dick.

Pierce closed his eyes, willing himself not to explode from the barely there touch. She got curious then, her hands rubbing up and down his hard length beneath his jeans. The seam of the zipper was oddly arousing, and he dropped his head back and moaned before touching her wrist.

"You see what you do to me? Fuck, I'm about to come like some teenager on his first date."

"Then why don't we finish?" she asked huskily, and it took every ounce of willpower he possessed to hit pause.

"Fuck baby, this is so hard—"

"I know," she grinned, and he barked a laugh.

"Ha ha. That's what she said," he growled playfully, plucking her hand off his cock and nibbling her fingers. "Look, I am stopping now because I want more than just this one night, pretty girl. You get what I am saying?" he asked.

Toni cocked her head, her eyes glittering gold with her Lioness. Pierce held his breath until she smiled, then he exhaled. That smile she gifted him with was absolutely heart-stopping, but somehow it got his beating again.

You are done, boy. She got you now.

"Thank you for that," Toni said, her voice husky with emotion. "Um, is it alright if I stay right here?" she asked, tucking her feet under her legs, and leaning on him.

"You better. If you move, I'll just follow you, anyway," he told her, only half teasing.

He pressed play and tried to focus on the show, but that was impossible. Watching a movie with the worst case of blue balls he'd ever had in his life was something Pierce never intended to do again. Not after tenth grade, anyway.

"Are you sure you're alright?" she asked, turning her head as the movie played in the background.

"Never better," he smiled tightly.

"You know, it's been a long time for me. I appreciate you going slow."

"And that right there makes all this worth it," he whispered, kissing her temple, and tucking her in close.

An hour later, the credits were rolling, and Pierce was still hard as stone. Didn't matter though, his discomfort was nothing compared to how good it felt just to hold her. His Tiger chuffed, content for the first time in a very long time.

He exhaled and stretched his free arm, looking down to see Toni had fallen asleep curled up against him. Damn, she really was the prettiest woman he'd ever seen. At some point during the evening, she had wiped off her makeup and braided her hair.

Fresh and clean, with her face relaxed in slumber, Toni looked like an angel. Either Pierce was the luckiest SOB in the whole damn world, or he was in big trouble with this one. Maybe both. Either way, he would not leave her on the couch.

He was already resigned to a night of discomfort, also known as *epic-blue-balls-itis*, but he would make sure his mate was tucked into bed safe and sound. Pierce paused as he stood, lifting her in his arms. Mate. The word had come so easily to his mind. But it felt right. He stared at her sleeping form and tested it out again.

Mate. Mine. Yesssss, the Tiger hissed.

Pierce's heart filled with emotion, and he closed his eyes, thanking the gods, Uncle Uzzi, Hunter, everyone he could think of for the chance to know this wonderful woman. He could already replace that word know with another four letter word starting with the letter l but was early days yet.

They had all the time in the world, and after what she'd been through with her ex and was still going through at work, he figured she deserved it. He walked her to the main bedroom, already having given that one up to her.

The cabin had a second, smaller one, and Pierce was fine sleeping in that one until their relationship progressed. Maybe it was the lawyer in him that didn't mind him taking his time. Then again, the hunt was just as important to his beast. But this felt bigger than a hunt. This felt like nothing he'd ever experienced.

Pierce balanced her on his leg and pulled the covers down, placing her gently on the sheets. Unable to resist, he bent and kissed her temple one more time, tucking her in. When he got to the door, he heard her whisper his name in sleep, and he stopped and closed his eyes. Forcing himself to leave the room was difficult, but he did it.

Barely.

Chapter Six

"Oh, come on! Not again, you big, dumb, blockhead!"

Pierce woke with a start to the sound of grunting, growling, and raised voices. Okay, *one* raised voice. He blinked his eyes, shaking his head before jumping out of bed.

"That's mine!" the voice said again,

What the heck was going on? Still stuck in that place between dream and sleep—and it had been a very good dream about a certain dark-haired temptress with glowing golden eyes and a body that made a man want to drop to his knees and beg at her feet for any crumb she'd be willing to give.

Fuck. One day with her, and he was losing his mind. His dick was so hard, the head was already peeking out of his boxer briefs. He stalked over to the window and just about lost his mind.

"Let go!" another shout sounded, this one closer to his window.

Pierce shook his head and walked to the window, and his jaw just dropped. Outside, in the tiniest pair of shorts he'd ever seen with a matching racer-back sports bra, was Toni. The sun was barely up, but the woman looked as though she was coming back from a hike or a run, or something.

When had she gone out? Why didn't she wake him? Why didn't his Tiger wake him? Pierce growled, annoyed at himself.

Worse than the fact she had gone traipsing through the damn forest in the dark hours before dawn was, despite leaving the cabin by herself, Toni was no longer alone. She had company. Big, furry, snarly, capable of maiming, if not killing, company.

"You dumb bear, I said let go!" she yelled.

Pierce's eyes bugged out of his head at the bear that was trailing behind her. Oh, he was not just any bear. It was the same fucker from yesterday. The stupidly big animal was hot on her heels. He nudged her camel backpack, catching it between his teeth.

Dammit.

The fucking bear was pulling on it, and Toni was still strapped in.

"Knock it off, you dolt!" she yelled, but the beast was having too much fun shaking her like a rag doll.

Pierce didn't even think. He opened the window roaring as he jumped down, shifting on the way. His Tiger burst forth, shredding his underwear, and forcing the shift faster than ever.

His animal was angry beyond reason. The bear released her backpack and pushed her out of the way, as if he was the one coming to Toni's defense and not Pierce.

What. The. Fuck.

The Tiger roared, swiping at the bear with his sharp claws. The bear growled back. The animal pawed at the ground and charged him. Good, he could finish the beast and have a snack. His Tiger snarled hungrily.

"Hey, stop! Pierce, no! And you, back off! STOP!" Toni shouted, jumping between them.

Pierce could not believe it. Was the woman insane? She just jumped between his big ass Tiger and a freaking bear.

Not a tiny baby bear, but a full-grown adult male. And he was huge! Completely wild, too. The bear wasn't some little house pet. Pierce could not believe it.

He was angry and scared. Didn't she care about her safety? He sure fucking did. And he was about to shift to tell her so when the damndest thing happened. Toni turned her back on his Tiger and faced the bear.

"What did I say? Huh? I told you, you could only join me if you behaved. *Only* if you *behaved*! Now, back off. Go on. Shoo," she said, pointing to the woods.

The black bear let out a mournful bellow, pawing the ground before backing away. One more sad look at Toni, who was beautiful if unrelenting if the fact she still pointed at the woods said anything, and the animal lumbered away.

"What the hell was that?" Pierce shouted, chest heaving as he shook off the remnants of his shift.

Fuck.

He hated switching forms so quickly. All Shifters did. It hurt like hell and then there was the aftermath. Tender skin, chills wracking his body, aching bones, and sore muscles—unpleasant, to say the least. Shifting wasn't for the faint of heart, that was for sure.

"What the hell was what?" she answered with a question.

"The bear, Toni! The big bear trying to eat you! Again!" he pointed to where the lumbering monster had gone off.

"Who? Yogi? He was not trying to eat me," she retorted, shrugging out of her backpack.

"Toni, that bear is a wild animal," he said, willing himself to be patient.

He was trembling still, with leftover adrenaline. Part of him wanted to shake her, the other part wanted to kiss her silly, run his hands over her body and make sure she was whole. The woman was trying to give him a goddamned heart attack.

"I know he is an animal, Pierce. We're animals, too," she said, leaving out the *no duh*, but he could still hear it in her voice.

"We're more than that, pretty girl," he replied, shaking his head in awe of her.

"Dang it, he tore my camel back," Toni muttered, shaking water out of the little plastic bladder inside the thing.

"What time did you leave? I thought you didn't go in for all this outdoorsy stuff," he said, rubbing his head.

"I don't know. It was still dark, besides I told you

I don't normally do vacations. My sisters got me this camel back thingy for hiking so I thought I would try it," she explained, walking past Pierce to get inside the cabin.

She was blushing, a pretty pink color he wasn't sure came from embarrassment or exertion. Either way, damn, she was cute, standing there in that outfit and guzzling water straight from a liter bottle she took out of the fridge.

"What's the matter with you?" she asked, one eyebrow raised.

Christ, he was so fucked.

"Toni, you could have been hurt, or worse," he explained, hands on his hips.

"Pierce, I'm a freaking Lioness. Besides, that bear loves me. He was waiting in the tree line for me and followed me all over the mountain like a puppy. Oh my gods, were you worried?" she asked, and her face lit up like a Roman candle.

"Who me? Worried. Nah," he mumbled, rubbing the back of his neck.

"Pierce? Did you think that old bear was gonna get me?" she teased some more, stalking him across the room.

Her grin was wide, and she was preening.

Dammit. She was right. He was worried. Might as well admit it, he figured.

"Dammit. Of course, I was worried, Toni. He's a wild animal, not a Shifter. You can't predict his actions. I was asleep. What if he attacked when you were too far for me to hear?" he muttered.

Fuck. Was he crazy? Or was she?

He felt foolish, irritable, and horny all at the same time—*and now it was showing, dammit.*

"You know, I think it's cute you worried about me," she told him, leaning up to drop a sweet, sexy as fuck kiss on his lips.

Pierce just fucking melted. Toni's body was so warm, and she smelled fantastic as she pressed herself against him and pushed her tongue into his mouth. He growled, taking her offered kiss and giving it back to her.

There was something deeply erotic about standing there, only their mouths locked together. He was too afraid to touch her at the moment. He was so wound up, Pierce was liable to take her against the counter. Toni sighed, stepping back too damn soon. His brows furrowed as his gaze followed her, and Toni, pretty girl that she was, was still grinning.

"Boner," she pointed out in a singsong voice, and

Pierce closed his eyes, unable to stop a chuckle from escaping.

"It's not polite to notice," he mock-scolded her.

Pierce shook his head, eyes still shut tight. If he looked at her now, it would all be over.

"Um, that thing is like a yardstick. How could I miss it?" Toni asked, her throaty laugh making his dick even harder.

Dammit, she had the perfect little mouth. All plump lips and pouty. He could just imagine those things wrapped around his cock—*ohmyfuckinggod, his dick was never going down.*

Pierce groaned. He flashed his eyes at hers once, then went back to reciting multiplication tables.

"Aww, come here, baby," she whispered, and he liked the nickname on her lips.

Toni put the water bottle down on the counter and ambled back over to him. This little dance of hers, within reach then not, was driving him mad. Her cheeks were still pink and those gold eyes of hers sparkled with mischief.

Pierce had never seen anything so dang pretty in his entire life. His heart thudded in his chest, speeding like a runaway train. He swallowed audibly as she ran her fingernails up his arms and over his shoulders, leaning up to place soft kisses on his cheeks and chin, then finally, one more on his tense lips.

Peaches, she always tasted like peaches to him, and sunshine, and honey.

Fuck, he loved honey. Loved it all. Loved her?

No. It was too soon for that, but his Tiger did not give a fuck. The animal was purring inside of him, dammit, and all because of her.

Mine.

"Thank you for rescuing me," she whispered.

"You don't need anyone to do that, pretty girl," he said, trying so damn hard to stop himself from grabbing her.

It was the wrong time for that. Pierce wanted her to trust him. To trust them. And whatever her past dealings with men, he could tell she'd gotten the wrong end of it. Yeah, she was brainy and beautiful and should be walking around like the queen of Sheba, but whenever she thought no one was looking, Pierce saw vulnerability.

It was the shy, tender part of her she kept so close, hidden from others, that he craved. Oh, he wouldn't coax it out of her. Wouldn't steal it. No, he wanted her *to want* to give it to him.

So, yeah, he could be patient. Her brows furrowed as she stepped back, head cocked as she watched him with curiosity in her Lioness' stare.

Ooooh, this kitty was so very pretty.

He wrestled with his own beast for control, reminding himself he was in this for the long haul. Toni was going to be so damn surprised when he stuck to her like glue after this getaway. He knew she wasn't there yet.

Toni didn't realize what she'd done with her big eyes and sexy kisses, but she'd won him over. Hell, she didn't even have to try.

Maybe that's what love was. Maybe it was falling with no effort at all, knowing someone was waiting to catch you in the end. But not just catch you. Maybe it was trusting that someone to catch you and let go when you needed to stand on your own.

To be there to listen to your problems, but not always try to fix them. That was gonna be hard on him. He was a fixer by nature. But Toni didn't need that from him. She was strong and tough, so damn smart. And fun. He never laughed so much as he did with her.

Oh yes, he knew she was it for him. Pierce was going to work so hard to get her to love him. He was gonna be there when she fell. He was gonna catch her and hold her up, let her go when she wanted to stand on her own. He was going to cheer her on and encourage her.

He just wanted to be there for all of it. Because he *wanted* to be. Not just needed to. Maybe that was the real test of true love. The wanting to be there part.

"I am taking a shower," he mumbled. "Mind your manners, pretty girl, and no bears while I am gone."

His thoughts were getting too heavy, and he was still pre-coffee this morning. Toni was watching him, and he winked, wanting to lighten the mood. He used two hands to cover his still hard as stone dick as he walked past.

"Hey, Pierce, what are we doing today so I know how to dress?" she asked as he walked off.

He could feel her eyes on him, and he paused, but only turned his head.

"I'm taking you someplace fun. Wear a bathing suit," he told her and winked.

"A surprise?" she asked.

"A surprise," he told her, having just decided where to bring her.

"Alright! I have got the perfect bikini I brought with me just in case there was swimming. Oh, and Pierce?" she continued when he started walking again.

"Yeah?"

"You have really nice *assets*."

Toni smirked, eyebrows wagging, while she checked out his butt. Pierce went cross-eyed. Trying to be a gentleman around this female was gonna kill him, for sure.

But what a way to go!

Chapter Seven

MAVERICK PRIDE

T he weather had cleared up, and it was beginning to look a lot like summer in the woods surrounding the cabin.

Finally.

The sky was a bright and brilliant blue and the sun a big, buttery ball in the sky. Its light shone through the beautiful window wall, painting everything with its golden hues. Outside, the woods held a variety of trees that lent themselves to a million different shades of green. It was like gazing at a living work of art.

The shades ranged from the palest lime of the young vines creeping up the shed behind the cabin to the deeper green of the needles covering the tall evergreens. Birds whistled gaily. The tiny scurrying sounds of forest mice, squirrels, and chipmunks running their morning errands were distant though chipper.

She couldn't blame them for wanting to go out into the world. It was a beautiful day, and Toni was in a fantastic mood. Seeing Pierce jump out a window, shifting to his beautiful beast just to save her, however unnecessarily, was really just an awesome way to start the day.

When was the last time a man had dared do something like that for her? Besides him. Just yesterday, in fact.

Hot, sexy, protective man.

Toni was used to taking care of herself. She was entirely capable, too, but that didn't mean it wasn't nice to have someone give a crap. So far, this little vacation plan of Uncle Uzzi's was entirely worth it. Hell, she hadn't even thought about work since yesterday.

Of course, now that she did, she walked over to her dresser and grabbed her cell phone. Typically, she would have dozens of work related messages waiting for her. Now, there were only a few. Sighing, she swiped her finger across the screen and opened the messenger app.

Adrianna

Yo, sis, how's it going? Did you get any (insert eggplant emoji)?

Toni rolled her eyes and saw her other sisters had been added to the chat. The last time they did this, the Golden girls had gotten up to all sorts of snarky hijinks. She bit her lip, not wanting to share anything just yet.

Annabeth

Yeah. We want some deets! Did Uncle Uzzi deliver or what?

Ariella

You guys, don't be rude. Toni, you don't have to tell us anything. But since there is a sister code and all, I feel you would be breaking it if you did not confide something...

Adrianna

Yeah. So, like I asked already, did you get any D I C K? (insert eggplant emoji)

Toni snorted a laugh. Her sisters were incorrigible. True, they did tell each other everything, but this was still so new. Oh yeah, she got picked up a lot. Shifters being total horn-dogs, that was to be expected. But after Stefan, she'd steered clear of any and all males.

So, Toni was not exactly batting a thousand when it came to men, and she wasn't sure she wanted to reveal anything yet. What if she jinxed it? Tapping her fingernails on her thigh, she decided to give them something. This was still so new, she needed to tread carefully, or they would home in on her like heat-seeking missiles.

Antonetta

Heyyyyy. Okay, so I am not ready to spill any deets, but yes, Uncle Uzzi delivered. Pierce McDowd is a total hottie and sweetheart.

Adrianna

OMG. You're in love!

Annabeth

Don't be ridiculous. It's been five minutes since she met him.

Ariella

Excuse me, sis, but how long after you met Hank were you in love?

Annabeth

Eat my fur, Ari! Oooh, but really, how is my baby niece doing?

Adrianna

Could be a nephew, AB. You know Wolves tend to sire male cubs. So we might be looking at a puppy.

Ariella

Do not call my unborn child a puppy! Besides, Dire Wolves call them cubs, too.

Antonetta

OMG. You girls never shut up. Okay. I'm going. He has a surprise for me.

Adrianna

Hey Toni, you know, you didn't even ask about work. I guess he really is special, huh? Good for you.

T oni gasped. Adrianna was right. She hadn't even thought about work in the past twenty-four hours. Grinning like mad, she closed the chat for now and went to shower and dress.

When she finished, she saw Pierce busily packing them a picnic lunch. He'd said he had a surprise for Toni, and the only hint he gave her was to wear a bathing suit, but she wanted to contribute. So, she made a bag with a blanket and towels, some sunscreen, and a wireless speaker so they could listen to music.

She was thinking there must be some sort of creek or something within walking distance, but when she went outside to meet him, she stopped short. Hunky Pierce was wearing a pair of shorts that stopped a good three inches above his knee, revealing thick, muscular thighs, and he was attaching the picnic basket and a small cooler to the back of some sort of tricked out golf cart.

"What the heck is that?" she asked, trying hard not to stare at him like he was meat.

Why? We like meat. Yummy, her lioness supplied unhelpfully.

"Hey, pretty girl."

Pierce greeted her with a lopsided grin on his oh-so-handsome face, as he walked the motorized death trap closer to her. Despite being a Lioness, Toni was not exactly a sporty kind of girl.

She might try hiking, sure, walking and even swimming every once in a while. But the truth was, she preferred things like movies and music, books especially to being outdoors.

Gah. What if she messed this up? Shifters were usually sporty and up for anything, but not Toni. She was a cautious kitty.

"Seriously, um, what is that?"

"This? Haven't you ever been on an ATV?"

"Um, no, not really," she murmured, worrying her lower lip.

The seats were side by side, but there were no doors, no roof. What the heck was she supposed to hold on to? As if he could read her mind, Pierce stood up and gestured her over. It moved her that he would stop what he was doing and take the time to explain it to her.

Toni was in no way lacking in the comprehension department. She was plenty smart, if inexperienced at certain things. Still, it was a rare thing in her world for a man to notice when she was uncomfortable. Not just that, but to care enough to set her at ease. Like he was studying every expression, and he was paying attention to them, well, to her.

I am noticing you, too, Pierce McDowd.

"Ah, well, no worries if this is your first time. I promise to be gentle," he said with a wink.

God, he was sexy. It was like flirting with the star quarterback when she was in high school. And wouldn't you know it? Toni giggled like a damn schoolgirl.

Get a grip. Be cool.

That was old Toni talking, though. This Toni, the one she discovered in the last day, did not want to be cool at all. She wanted to be playful and giddy, to experience the feelings she was actually feeling. She did not want to hide beneath a smooth façade. Toni wanted to be real with him.

And wasn't that saying something? Since when did she want to show anyone the wizard behind the curtain? Most of the time, she was closed off, tight-lipped. But not with him. The sexy Tiger was breaking down all her walls.

He was melting the ice around her heart. Chiseling away at all her barriers. Pierce was like pure sunshine. This constant, primal source of power, energy, and heat. Ooh, she liked his heat. She wanted to bask in it with him.

No more ice queen. He was defrosting her with his fire. Smexy as all get Tiger Shifter with his crooked grin, honest words, and killer abs. He was the whole package, and she was completely intrigued by him. Toni was a curious kitty by nature, and he was just so multi-faceted.

Everything he said and did was a surprise. She kept waiting for the reveal. For his true colors to show. Man who looked like that, well, he must be egotistical or conceited, but no. Not Pierce. He was sweet and kind, and that panty-melting smile of his made her want to do deliciously dirty things with him.

Yes, please.

"You went quiet," he observed. "Everything okay?"

"Yeah. I'm good. Um, tell me about this death trap," she said, and he barked a laugh.

"Okay, well, this baby here is an all-terrain vehicle, and, as you can see, there are two seats, plenty of room for the picnic basket, cooler, and bag, and look, seat belts," he said with an air of confidence she truly admired.

"So, you can drive this thing, is what you're telling me?" she hedged.

"You betcha. Come on, hop in."

Toni bit her lip as she circled the mini death trap. Truth was, she didn't do much hopping. Her tendency to over analyze situations like this lent itself to very little spontaneity in her life.

Fine, she was being a wuss. As a Lioness, she could totally admit that to herself. But there was no way she was letting the striped behemoth of a male watch her wimp out.

"If you want, we can do something else," he said kindly, offering her an out without being a dick about it.

How did the man manage to be so smooth, sexy, and sweet, too? Toni was going to need a mini fan, like one of those things with the water bottle attached they sold at theme parks, or something like it, to cool herself off if he kept this up.

"Toni? Wanna skip this?" he asked, concern marring his brow.

Uh uh. No way. It was time to put on her big girl panties.

"No way, besides this looks safe enough, and you did mention seat belts," she said, more for her benefit than his.

"I wouldn't put you in this thing if it wasn't safe, pretty girl. Scout's honor."

Pierce saluted her, giving her that sexy lopsided grin of his. She smiled back, unable to help herself. He was definitely one of the good ones. Those mystery males other women talked about, and two of her own sisters had managed to nab.

"You say that, and yet," she murmured, wincing at her own cowardice.

"Would I lie?" he asked, eyebrows raised.

"No, I don't think you would," she murmured, and his gaze softened as he looked down at her.

Oh yeah, Pierce was good. Kind. Sexy. Patient. Irresistible. And those were just some of the words she was starting to associate with him. Lions and Tigers didn't really play together in the wild. But in the Shifter world, they played nicely, or so Toni was learning.

She circled the tiny vehicle again. No doors. Ugh. That meant she would have to heft her fluffy ass up and onto the seat. Oh boy. Guess she would be embarrassing herself, after all.

"Do you trust me?" Pierce said, suddenly right behind her.

Toni startled, gasping, and holding a hand over the pounding in her chest. She turned her head, her pulse running wild. Her heart was doing its best to beat right out of her chest, and the damn male seemed to know it.

Pierce's aqua eyes glittered down at her and this close, she saw specks of emerald weaving through them. His cheeks held a smattering of shadow, and he looked rough and masculine, and oh, so tempting.

Dangerously sexy.

"Yes, I do," she replied, shocked she actually meant it.

Pierce's chest rumbled with his growl, and she realized he liked her reply. Like it meant something to him to have her trust. Warmth filled her, reflecting the heat in his unwavering gaze. Never had a man met her eyes so steadily, and she had to admire him for that.

The Golden sisters had reputations for being maneaters. But that was all just rumor and innuendo. But Toni had clung to that rep, using it like armor to push men away. Especially after her ex.

That guy had done a number on her, and for the first time, she saw why.

Stefan was a manipulator. A liar and a cheat. A no good, mean, rude, and self-centered person.

Pierce was his polar opposite. He was a nurturer. A giver, not a taker. He was a builder, literally.

He builds people up just as easily as he builds cabins, she thought with a grin.

Pierce just gave and gave and gave. He didn't push. Uncle Uzzi had sure found the right guy for her, and thanking her lucky stars, Toni realized she actually felt happy right here and now.

Mine, her Lioness purred, and Toni breathed a little easier.

Chapter Eight

Maybe her animal was never broken. Maybe she'd just been eager to find someone to be with and that was why she'd set her sights on Stefan. Toni couldn't hold a grudge.

Not any longer. After all, she and her Lioness had to live together. And if her kitty was making statements like that about Pierce, something she never actually did with Stefan, then maybe the beast was smarter than she thought.

Mine.

Yeah, he felt like hers. But she wasn't about to shout it from the rooftops and scare him off. Not yet anyway. She was eager to spend time with Pierce, getting to know him, and showing him the real her, the one she kept hidden. Toni didn't want to wear armor with him.

For the first time, she wanted to be herself, to allow her vulnerability to show. Yes, it was soon, but they were Shifters. This feeling of hope and excitement, this was what was missing with Stefan. This was what she'd been waiting to feel all her life.

Pierce held out his hand, and all manner of teasing fled from his eyes. He seemed to hold his breath, waiting for her to decide. She swallowed hard, then took his proffered hand, using it to leverage herself into the vehicle.

Her Lioness already recognized him for what he was. The she-beast knew it, and she purred with the knowledge. Yep. Even her kitty was eager to spend the day with him.

"Eek!"

Her foot slipped on the rail she was using to hoist herself up, but he had her waist, and he waited for her to regain her footing instead of just manhandling her. She was grateful even as she muttered, wondering how graceless she must have looked bumbling into the thing.

"There you go, pretty girl," he said with a grin.

"Get buckled and I'll get you where we're going, safe and sound," he growled in reply.

Truth. Truth. TRUTH.

There was a path through the woods behind the shed where he'd pulled the ATV from, and Toni smiled in delight. She'd gone the other way on her hike that morning.

"I completely missed this trail this morning," she said over the hum of the engine.

"Did you? This part of the woods is full of trails. Some we made when we were building up here. Others from years of the Pride camping up here, before we had cabins," he replied.

"No cabins? Yikes. Well, I'm glad you all built them. I don't really do camping," she said, laughing at his shocked expression.

"You don't camp?" he asked, his eyebrows raised to his hairline.

The man had gorgeous hair. Thick, straight, glossy, and dark with one lock falling perfectly onto his forehead. Sexy, hot guy hair was a total thing for her kind. All the Lion males in the Pride were going to be jealous of a Tiger, she mused, her fingers itching to muss it.

"Mmm hmm," she told him. "No tents for me. I

need a mattress and indoor plumbing. Non-negotiable."

"You're one of those high maintenance women," he said, a teasing note in his voice. "So noted, fair lady."

Toni laughed aloud and Pierce nodded his head, feigning seriousness. That didn't last long, and he was chuckling right along with her a moment later. Gosh, this was easy. Easy and comfortable. She liked it. She liked him.

"So, where are you taking me, kind sir?" she asked, tucking her hair behind her ears.

It was whipping wildly in the wind as they raced through the trees. Normally, she would be up in arms over the state of it, but right then, she didn't care. It felt good, letting her hair down literally and figuratively.

She must have looked a mess, with her hair flying around like that, but Pierce didn't seem to mind. His lazy smile was sexy and complimentary as he raked her with that aqua gaze of his.

"Don't worry. You'll like it, I promise," he said, and his smile went so bright it dazzled her.

Toni relaxed back into the seat and tried not to flinch at the speed with which they were moving through the forest. Traveling to Maverick Point from Blue Valley, Toni spent a lot of time looking at the peak of the mountain, but it was wild to think she was actually on it.

"We are on the mountain, right?" she asked.

"Yep. We are a few miles up the base of Mount Maverick. You can hike up to the top, but it's not really for beginners. Our animals might get farther along than us, actually," he replied.

After about twenty minutes, Pierce slowed the ATV down, rounding a bend that had been blocked from view by tall trees and bushy shrubs. She identified oaks and black walnuts, a few scraggly pines, but Toni wasn't exactly nature girl.

"It's a lake!" she shouted, pointing at the crystal clear body of water.

"Yep. We can swim in it, it's naturally filtered by those floating rafts you see out in the middle there. The vegetation is good for the lake. Closer to the shore, we roped off the main swimming area, and there is another filter there to clear it even more for swimmers. The Pride mamas prefer it when their cubs don't come out of the water looking like swamp thing," he teased.

Toni grinned right along with him. She could just

imagine how some moms, especially the young ones, felt protective and concerned over their young. She and her sisters had grown up pretty wild, though. Her own mother never cared about a mess, and she and her sisters and brother would have torn a lake up as cubs.

"Wow, so wait. Can you just do all that to a lake on a mountain? No consequences or permission needed?" she asked, curious about his Pride.

And wasn't that new, too? Toni, though inquisitive by nature, was rarely concerned with other Shifter groups. But if the Fates had paired her up with a Tiger, well, it seemed the thing to do. Asking him questions, learning the ins and outs of his pride and his life.

This felt good. Safe, yet exciting. New. It felt new, and that was good.

"The Pride owns this land. Actually, this lake was put here by us," he said, putting the ATV into park along a strip of gravel.

They did not exit the vehicle right away, and she was glad. She wanted to finish this conversation. Toni was learning so much about him, she was too engrossed to stop.

"So, you all just made a lake?" she asked, totally shocked.

"Yeah, people do it all the time. We put this in right about the time we built the cabins. This place is a retreat for the Pride, and for other Shifters who get our Neta's permission," he explained, surprising her further.

"Wow. This is really wonderful. I mean, I did not know this even existed, and I lived in New Jersey my whole life."

"Well, communication between Shifter groups is all but nil. We've been working with the Shifter Council to increase talks between different groups. This place was designed with the idea it could serve as host for different groups to come together, explore relationships, discuss business in a peaceful, friendly, and safe environment."

"Wow. Your Neta must really be incredible. I mean, this is really a wonderful idea," she said, looking around with newly opened eyes.

"Hunter Maverick is the best man I know, but uh, well, actually, I made the plans for this retreat," he murmured, and his cheeks went all ruddy.

Sweet, sexy, bashful, too. What other surprises do you have in store for me, Pierce McDowd?

"You mean the architectural plans?" she asked, confused.

She knew he worked for Maverick Development,

which was a construction company. She was not sure exactly what it was he did there, but if it involved building this place, she was definitely impressed.

"Sure, I helped with part of the design, but I meant the idea of using this retreat for peace talks as neutral ground for different Shifter groups was my idea. Maverick Development is really the only Shifter run company of its kind in this area, as such, it makes sense to negotiate contracts with other Shifters who would not be surprised by the speed or size of the work we can actually do. But those kinds of deals need privacy to work through. This place offers that," he stated and hopped out of the ATV.

He was around to her side, hand extended, before she had a chance to even get unbuckled. Gods, he had good manners. She loved that, loved the way he treated her. Toni's cheeks were burning by the time she got awkwardly out of her seat.

"Thank you."

"Anytime, pretty girl," he murmured, touching her chin before turning to get their things.

"So, you came up with that whole thing for your Pride's company? I mean, wow, Pierce. That is really something," she murmured, surprised, and even more impressed.

"Thanks. It's part of why I went to law school. To handle the contracts and negotiations," he told her nonchalantly as he grabbed the cooler and the bag from the back.

"Hold the phone. Law school? You're a lawyer? Wait, I thought you worked construction," Toni said, following him.

She offered to carry the bag, but he shook his head and winked. A lawyer and a gentleman. Ha! It sounded like one of her romance books. The man was just full of surprises.

"Can't a man do both?" he asked, and his cheeks went a deeper shade of red.

Oh, he was good. Secretively smart, sexy as sin boy.

"Come on. Let's set up the picnic," he murmured.

Toni felt dizzy with all this new information she was gleaning about him. Dizzy and intrigued. Very, very intrigued. She took a moment to fan herself when he wasn't looking.

Yowza.

The man was doing things to her she'd never experienced with barely a touch. Kindling fires of desire, that's what he was doing. Every glance, every light brush of his fingertips as he guided her down the graveled path to the sandy shore.

"We drive up sand at the start of every season

here, to fill in where the weather or animals eroded it," he told her as he set the bag and cooler down.

"Oooh, so soft sand. I was worried about mud and twigs hurting my butt," she said, only half-teasing.

"I promise if anything hurts your butt, I will kiss it and make it better."

"I bet you would, dirty boy," she tsked. Pierce chuckled and shrugged, clearly not refuting his statement.

"Anyway, it's really great," she replied honestly as she helped him spread open a blanket.

They sat down, side by side, and even that surprised her. She thought he would sit opposite her, but the big, sexy man just sprawled out like the big Cat he was right beside her. Every time he moved, he touched her.

Oh, nothing blatant. He was not groping or acting leery in any way. They were tiny touches. Just a light brush of his leg or his hand against her skin. Enough to send her system into hyperawareness mode. Those almost touches were driving her mad, amping up her desire for him.

Pierce was just so damn cute. He talked to her, listened when she spoke, and made her dish without hesitation. He was relaxed, charming, going into the basket he had packed for food when her stomach growled. He handed her a cup of fruit salad and a big, bready bagel loaded with lox and cream cheese.

"This is delicious," she said, taking hearty bites.

Toni was never going to hide that part of her, and Pierce seemed to love the fact she ate with gusto. They ate and shared stories. It was like he was really interested in everything she had to say. That was something she never really encountered.

"You did all that for Annabeth and her mate?"

"Well, I volunteered for the assignment to check on her. She's my sister. Besides, her heat was coming at the most inopportune time. She needed help. We Goldens stick together."

"That's awesome. You must be the best sister, hands down. I bet your sisters say so all the time."

"Hardly," she snorted.

"Agree to disagree, but really, I see what you are saying, and I get it, really. The females in our Pride have to deal with that as well. You know, there is talk of a human scientist who is mated to a feline Shifter, they are part of some elite Shifter group, I forget which. Anyway, he's said to be making advances in a sort of tonic to help stave off a heat cycle."

"Yes! His mate is one of the Guardians of Chaos. Tough group of supes. Unfortunately, the tonic requires each patient to come in and do a blood panel. There is a waitlist for consultations a mile long. I was lucky to have mine over a year ago," Toni said, then froze.

Oh shit. She had not meant to confess so much at once, but maybe this was a good thing. She cleared her throat and tucked her hair behind her ears, not meeting his eyes just yet.

"So, you got in? That's good. So, you are taking the heat suppressant?" he asked, curious but not judgy. "Shit. I'm sorry, Toni, that is none of my business," he added quickly.

Interesting. Most males had views about this sort of thing, but Toni would be damned if anyone was going to tell her how to take care of her own body. That was her business. No one else's.

"No, it's okay. I brought it up. And yes, to answer your question, I am taking the heat suppressant they made for me."

"You don't have to say another word about it, pretty girl. Your body, your choice," he murmured, and she heard it in his voice.

Truth.

Pierce told her nothing but the truth. He smiled

at her then, and it was so bright it was blinding. That smile said a lot to her. It told her he was okay with her choices. Even more than that. He did not judge her or question her choices. And he sure a shit didn't try to mansplain her own body to her—*thank fuck.*

He just listened, picked up his bagel and offered her a bite, which she took. He'd added EVOO to his food, and it really brought out the flavor of the salmon. Seeing her nod, he poured a drizzle across hers, and continued to eat while she spoke.

"I don't mind talking about it," Toni said. "Humans go on birth control all the time, and it is no big deal. But when a Shifter does, the whole supernatural community goes in an uproar."

"Double standard," he said, nodding.

"Yep. When Logan Wells, that's the scientist's name, brought his discovery before the Council of Shifters, they were angry. They said he was interfering with nature. Then female Shifters started coming forward and explaining what it meant to them to be able to choose whether to go into their heat cycle, and after a while, that changed their point of view."

"I remember those talks. I was there," he said, surprising her further. "And I agree with you. Women should have a choice in who they mate and

119

have young with. My own mother went into her heat cycle when she was barely out of high school. She wound up mating the boy next door, and lucky for her, they fell in love," he told her with a small smile.

"Sounds like a dream, unfortunately, that's not the norm," Toni replied with a sad smile.

"I know. I had a cousin who wasn't so lucky," Pierce added darkly. "Her heat cycle hit her when she was away on a tour of Europe and the male who serviced her, well, he was not kind to women. He refused to let her return to the states, to her family and pride, and she, uh, she ended her life," he whispered.

"Oh no, Pierce, I am so sorry," Toni said, her heart hurting for him.

"I was very young. We weren't close, but still. It does something to you, having someone close to you hurt by something beyond your control. So, Toni, I am not judging you for your choices. I applaud them and I am glad you can make those decisions for yourself," he told her, and she saw more truth gleaming in his aqua-tinted gaze.

"Thank you. I appreciate that. You see, I didn't want to be at the mercy of biology for a few reasons," she said, opting for the whole truth. "I mean, I was just getting a promotion at work. But that wasn't the whole reason I wanted the suppressant. I wanted it, well, because of the man I was dating."

"Why? Was he pressuring you into having cubs?" he asked, and his voice had deepened.

"Yes, well, he wanted to claim me, and he wanted me to have cubs right away. He had this whole plan you see, and when I balked, he told me no one else would want me because I was so focused on my career."

"Name and address," Pierce growled.

"No," she laughed, stopping when she saw he was serious. "I mean, he was kinda right, Pierce, in a way. I worked eighty hours a week. Weekends, unpaid overtime, I mean, look at all I gave to EWLP. And for what? At the slightest hint of scandal or something off in my work, they send me packing. They wouldn't even let me help with the investigation into my activities. So, what good did I really do, working all those hours?"

Toni shivered. She frowned, staring out at the lake without really seeing it. Was this going to hurt them before they even started, she wondered. And it surprised her to realize she feared that. Toni didn't want to lose him.

"Did you love him?" Pierce asked.

Toni paused before answering. She was not expecting that question. Did she love Stefan? Her Lioness had wanted her to. At the time, Toni thought she might. But the answer was clear as a bell now.

"I thought I did, for like a minute, but no, I never loved him," she confessed, and damn, did that feel good letting that cat out of the bag?

"Did he love you?"

"No," she said, shaking her head. That admission came easy and fast. Too easy.

"I don't think he is capable of love, and I am not saying that to be mean," she explained.

"I didn't think you were," Pierce said softly.

"Actually, he made me feel like shit for not loving him. Like it was just a choice or something. He said I wasn't trying. But I was. I did try. It just wasn't there on either side. Finally, I asked him how could he love me and make me feel like that? Anyway, he did not like my answer."

After a pause, she went on, feeling it necessary to say the whole thing.

"I'm sorry, Toni. That sounds hard," Pierce said, brushing his finger against hers where they touched n the blanket.

"Staying would have been hard. Leaving was easy.

Stefan, that was his name, said I was a cold fish and would never have a better offer. He wanted me to let him mark me with his bite, to get off the heat suppressants so my cycle would get my she-Cat more involved, but I refused. I wanted to wait. But in a way, I guess he was right. I cared more about my job than him. So, there it is. My big red flag. Workaholic."

"Hey," Pierce replied, reaching out to touch her cheek with his fingertips. "First, I am sorry about whatever this whole thing is going on at work. Second, you being dedicated and hardworking is hardly a red flag. That asshole, Stefan, whose last name and address I would really, really like to have, had no right to make you feel bad about any of that. He had no right to tell you what to do with your body or how to do your job."

"Yeah? You think so?" she asked, feeling pretty raw at that moment.

"I know so, pretty girl. Any real man would have supported you and your efforts. And trying to bully you into accepting his claim? Fuck that guy, Toni. He wasn't worthy of you."

Toni could not even muster a reply. She gasped, eyes wide at the fierce confidence in Pierce's gaze. He believed every word he said, and he was right. He was so fucking right. And up until just then, she hadn't realized it.

"And last, about you being a cold fish? That guy didn't know what the fuck he was talking about."

"He didn't?"

"Hell no. All you have to do is look at me, and bam, instant boner. You light fires in my body with a glance, Antonetta Golden. Anytime you're ready to next level this, you let me know. I'll be waiting right here," he admitted.

Pierce gifted her with that sexy, lopsided grin that made her body positively ache with longing, and she inhaled slowly. Hot damn. She was flustered, hot and bothered, and he barely touched her. Was she ready to next level this, she wondered.

Maybe she wasn't a cold fish. Maybe Stefan really was an asshole.

"Damn straight, pretty girl. Nothing cold about you."

Fuck.

She must have said that part aloud. Toni glanced down at her hands, currently wrinkling the shit out of the blanket they were sitting on. She smoothed it out and nodded slowly, willing herself to calm down.

"Good to know," she whispered, her heart soaring with possibilities.

He was so smart and funny. Open and honest with her. She still couldn't wrap her head around everything she was learning about him. Lawyer, architect, construction worker. How many more interesting facets was Pierce McDowd hiding from her? She couldn't wait to find out.

After they finished eating, Toni walked to the edge of the lake. The sun was high in the sky now, the hottest time of day. She bit her lip and reached for the hem of the tank top she'd tossed on over her bikini.

"What are you looking at?" she asked, eyebrow raised as she paused mid pull.

"The sexiest damn woman I have ever seen in my life," he replied, eyes unblinking.

"Well, don't. I never took off my clothes for an audience before," she said with a breathless sort of giggle that was so not her.

"Why not?"

"Excuse me? Are you implying I should strip?"

"Hell no, I mean, yeah, if you want to. Shit. I have nothing against strippers, and if a person chooses to take their clothes off for whatever reason, more power to them. What I meant was you have absolutely no reason to hide from me," he growled, cheeks going ruddy again.

"I'm not sure what you are saying, Pierce, but I would really like you to explain,"

Toni held her breath, her hands still on the hem of her shirt. She wasn't fishing for compliments, but damn, he was on the verge of telling her something and she wanted to get it right.

Stefan had savaged her pride. Made her feel unwomanly and just plain unattractive. His lack of interest went beyond her own pleasure or needs. The male was a taker, and Pierce was his polar opposite.

Pierce was a giver. And maybe, just maybe, Toni was ready to receive.

"What I am trying so ineloquently to say is, look, if you want me to turn around, I will. But if I may, I would give my eyeteeth to watch you pull that top, and anything else you want, off your body," he murmured.

Toni blinked slowly. Without another word, she pulled the tank top completely off, next came her shorts. Pierce exhaled long and slow, his eyes eating her up, and she shivered in response to his hungry stare.

Standing in her two-piece, she felt too confined, too covered up. Her pulse raced and blood roared in her ears. She wanted him to see all of her.

So, what are you waiting for?

Her hands crept up to the strings around her neck, and holding his gaze, she tugged. The entire mountain seemed to go quiet as she let the bikini top drop and moved her fingers to the ties on either side of her bottoms. When that too had fallen, Toni stepped backwards, allowing the cool lake water to lap at her legs.

The moment was ripe with tension. She heard birds and animals skittering through the forest, but even those sounds fell away until all she could hear was the beating of her heart. She was about two seconds from tucking tail and running, but she held her ground.

Toni held Pierce's glittering gaze until the water reached her waist. Then, she sunk down, immersing herself in the aquatic paradise. The sound of fumbling footsteps followed by a loud splash reached her supernaturally enhanced auditory senses beneath the surface of the lake, and she grinned.

One second later, Pierce's hard mouth was pressed against her lips as his body crashed into hers with all the force of a hurricane. It was turbulent, scary, and sexy as fuck. Toni didn't have to worry, he had her.

Gods, did he have her as he turned them around in the water, his hard, muscled body wrapped around hers. Her lungs burned with the need to breathe, but this was more important than air. Pierce was more important than anything.

Mine.

Chapter Nine

I f Pierce died right then and there, he would die a happy Tiger.

Holy. Shiiiiiiit.

Watching Toni do her slow striptease without moving a muscle was a magic trick Pierce did not know he could pull off—*until he did*. Was it worth all those long seconds of muscle torture?

Fuck. Yes.

The woman was stunning. Long-limbed and curved like the goddess of love herself, Toni was a stunner. Her dark, glossy hair fell down her back in a velvet curtain. He gulped loudly, daydreaming about how good it would look spread across his crisp white sheets.

Did he say stunning? Oh, she was more than that.

Sassy. Lioness. Badass. Goddess. Keeper of his heart. Owner of his body. Love of his life. Mate. Mate. MATE.

His thoughts ran wild as he drank her in. From head to toe, Toni was breathtaking. Her skin was lightly tanned, smooth, and supple. She had a few tiny scars on her knees, speaking to the childhood she had briefly told him about. Scuffles with her siblings, and shenanigans and wild pranks.

Hell, he couldn't wait to learn how she got each one. Listening to her talk with that husky voice of hers was quickly becoming one of his favorite things. The woman could tell a story. Hell, she captured his attention, that was certain. She was so damn intriguing to him.

He wanted her secrets, would even beg her to give them to him if that's what it took. Hell. There was not much he wouldn't do for her already, and that was saying something.

Pierce was a hunter by nature, but Toni was not prey. She was something else. Something bigger than that. And right now, she was killing him.

She stood there naked as the day she was born. Her confidence filled the air, and that was a thing of pure beauty and power. The woman was giving him gifts he never expected to receive, allowing him to look his fill at her sumptuous body, and oh yeah, he looked.

How could he not? With her standing there brazen, bold, and so damn beautiful, with eyes that glowed gold, and lips begging to be kissed. Her name played over and over again in his mind, building in intensity.

Toni. Toni. Sexy Toni. My Toni.

A hint of a smile teased the corner of her lips as she backed into the water, knowing better than to turn her back on him. Pierce's entire body buzzed with energy. He was wound so tight, one wrong move and he would break into a billion pieces.

The second she was surrounded by the lake, the cold water stealing her from his covetous view, it was like a switch flipped in his brain.

What the fuck was he doing just sitting there?

One more second, then he was off. Standing up, Pierce kicked off his clothes, bumbling a little as one short leg got caught around his ankle. His Tiger roared, the monster practically shredding him from the inside out, demanding he go to her.

Mine. Mine. MATE.

Every second he spent with Toni was like a test

of his self-control. He'd never been the kind of guy to have throngs of women hanging on the sidelines. That was more Lance's style, but even he changed after meeting his fated mate, courtesy of one uber awesome Witch's magical mojo.

Uncle Uzzi had gone above and beyond, far as Pierce was concerned. Toni was amazing. Everything he learned about the sassy Lioness had him craving more. He was greedy for every tidbit she shared. He wanted more. He wanted it all.

And not just her body—though honestly, Pierce was fairly certain he was going to die if he didn't get to touch her soon. He wanted her so badly, he could taste it.

Peaches and honey, and mine. Fuck, yes, mine.

She was everything he had ever wanted in a mate. Strong, feisty, honest, and so beautiful, he could barely look away. He wanted to do everything right, but that was a tall order.

No one was perfect, right? Only she was perfect. At least, to him, she was. But would he measure up? He was a fuck up at work. His ambition all but nil lately.

Only now that he'd found her, well, it was creeping back in. He wanted to do better. He wanted to *be better* for himself and for her. Pierce pushed every single one of his doubts and misgivings down and out of his head.

They had no place here. Here, there was only the future, and it was filled with beautiful possibilities. He had the opportunity to be something to someone with Toni and he wanted that.

Want her. Right fucking now.

Diving into the lake, he found her with unerring accuracy. He pulled her to him, crashing his mouth to hers and pushing up till they broke the surface. Their bodies were slick with cool water, but he was burning up with desire.

Toni clung to him, her arousal permeating the air with her honey sweet musk. Pierce's growl was nonstop now. He could no more hush the beast than he could his need to touch and kiss every inch of the sumptuously soft female in his arms.

This felt good. Almost too good, but this was no fantasy. He never believed he would ever find someone to fit him as perfectly as Elissa fit Hunter, or complement him the way Jessica did Brayden, or Reg and Gretchen. So many of his Pride mates, his brothers in the Neta's Honor Guard, had found their true fated mates and were better for it.

It was all his Tiger wanted for months now, and Pierce could not contain his joy. He had found her.

She was here, and better than anything he could have imagined. His entire body vibrated with emotion and his Tiger's constant growl. The beast was dying to claim her, to sink his teeth into her skin and make her his in every way possible.

"Pierce," she moaned, wrapping her legs around his waist as he moved them to a mound of wide, smooth, flat rocks just around the west bank of the lake.

Every nibble and plucking kiss sent his nerves into overtime. She felt so good, warm, and pliable with every curve molding to his body.

"Fuck, I'm trying to go slow, but I don't think I can resist you any longer, *pretty girl*," he whispered the endearment that was not entirely accurate.

Toni was not just pretty. She was everything.

"Tell me you want this now. I'll stop if you want me to, but I have to know," he gasped, stopping their kiss long enough to get the words out.

"Don't you dare stop," she growled, amber eyes glowing as she pulled him down to her for another openmouthed kiss.

The woman wielded her tongue like a wizard, and Pierce was putty in her hands. Well, make that a whole lotta inches of hard as steel putty. Her appreciative moan had him growing even harder, and it was all he could do to keep up with her kiss. In and out, her tongue tantalized him in a rhythm as old as time, but each stroke and swipe were new with her, and Pierce was completely engrossed.

Fuuuucccccck.

She sighed into his mouth, the sound as sweet as honey peach flavor, and Pierce wanted more. More of her sighs. More of her kisses. More of everything. Just more. Her hands cupped his ass, and she squeezed before tracing her nails up his spine and back over his shoulders.

Spell weaver, he thought with wonder, as she continued to explore the contours of his body with searching hands. Pierce had never been particularly fond of this part of sex. He always felt like a piece of meat, as if his partner was sizing him up. Only, not with her.

They were not right for you, but she is, his Tiger growled.

Toni's hands worked like magic. Everywhere she touched sizzled and burned with desire. She reached between them, taking hold of his dick, and he just about died. Pierce squeezed his eyes shut, two seconds from exploding.

Don't you fucking dare, he scolded himself.

Barely back in control, he hissed a long, desperate

sigh as Toni opened her legs wider and fitted him to her entrance. His body was wound so tight, he could hardly get any air into his lungs. Pierce was drowning in her. Inch by inch, he pressed into her tight, hot sheath, swallowing her moan when his hips pressed into hers.

"Oh gods, you feel so good," she whispered, her voice laced with pure awe.

"It's you, Toni, all you," he whispered back, his forehead leaning against hers.

He waited a moment for her body to adjust to his girth and size. Then he moved, and the whole universe imploded on him. Everything, everyone just disappeared, and all he was, all he could see, hear, feel, touch, taste was her.

Toni was everything to him now. Oh, he was with her, right then and there. Moving to bring them both to a pinnacle he'd yet to experience, and he could not fucking wait. Pierce had been driving for this his whole damn life.

Mine. Mine. MINE.

His Tiger's understanding, simplistic though it might be, was in no way wrong. She was his, and he was stamping himself allover her, inside of her, every place he could touch. Antonetta Golden was so much more than even she knew.

Yes, she'd been dealt a bad hand, and true, she did not need anyone to pick her up and straighten it out. The woman was a fierce, kickass Lioness. Pierce was just the lucky sonovabitch who'd been fated to be with her.

He wanted to claim her already. But he knew he had to wait. Fighting back the burning of his gums, he rocked his hips, moving in tight, shallow thrusts against her needy little nubbin.

Toni clawed at his back, but he kept his pace steady. Refusing to rush what was bound to be the epitome of all his sexual experiences. Sexy, smoldering little temptress that she was, Toni reared up. Latching onto his neck with her lips and teeth, she sucked hard, and he was powerless to resist.

Fuck. Why would he even try?

He flipped them over, moving so he sat on the rock with her astride him. Toni moaned, clutching at his shoulders, rivulets of water streaming over her breasts and belly, shoulders and back. Her dark hair hung down in wet strands, and her heavy-lidded eyes glowed with her Lioness.

"Ride me," he commanded.

"I, I never—" she stammered.

"You can do it, baby. I bet you're so fucking good

at it," he growled, need making his voice impossibly deep.

Toni squeezed his hips with her thighs, watching him carefully as she started to move, tentatively at first, then with more confidence as she found her rhythm.

Fuck yes. He'd been right. She was good at this. Sooooo fucking good.

Her claw-tipped fingers gripped his shoulders, piercing the skin there, but he welcomed the bite of pain. She rocked and swiveled, sliding her tight little pussy up and down his dick.

Holy balls, he was gonna explode.

She moved faster, panting as she increased her pace. His own breathing was unsteady as Pierce explored her rocking body with a desperation he'd never felt. He was using his hands to memorize her flesh, every curve and peak, every dimple and dip.

Unable to resist, he thrust up, meeting her downward moves. Fuck, she was so good. So hot. So tight. So right. Yes, this was so right.

Toni's mouth opened in a soundless moan, and her back arched. Pierce took over, taking her hips and moving her up and down his cock. He felt the first ripples of her orgasm rock right through him, and, unable to stop the tide, he joined her.

Pleasure crashed into him, completely engulfing all his senses. Rather than slide out of her, Pierce continued to move, dragging out every single ripple and aftershock of pleasure he could for her body. Toni clung to him, mashing her lips to his as she shivered in the aftermath of pure pleasure.

Good. Mine. Mate.

The beast in him roared, begging him to stake his claim. But he ignored the animal. Toni deserved more than that. She deserved a choice, and he was going to make sure she had it.

"I-I never had. I mean, that was so, wow. That was just so wow," she whispered, still clinging to him, his mouth nibbling at hers.

"Yeah, pretty girl. It really was wow," he whispered back, cradling her close. "And it's just the beginning."

"Oh yeah?" she smiled against his mouth, still too sated to move off him just yet.

Good. he wanted her right there.

"You trying to get me addicted to you, Pierce?" she asked, her voice teasing but only slightly.

"Damn straight I am. Full disclosure, Miss Golden, I plan on keeping you right here with me, and I am going to fight dirty."

"Ha! Oh yeah, how's that?" she asked, more

teasing lightness in her voice, and he liked that. Very much.

"See, I'm going to spoil you rotten, love you so good, get you so used to feeling good with me, you are gonna crave it."

"Oh, so you're gonna trap me with good sex?"

"More than good sex, fantastic sex, thank you very much. But it's not a trap if you want to be here, right? And you will want to be here Toni because I know you feel it, too. Now, don't tense up," he murmured.

Pierce started kissing her temple and rubbing her back until she settled again. He waited until Toni was looking at him to continue.

"I swear, I'll never try to run roughshod over you. I will never tell you what to do with your body or give you ultimatums. I want to be with you, but at your pace. You hold the reins here. You control how fast and far we move."

"Yeah? You okay with giving me control?"

"Hell yeah. My Tiger is dominant, but he's yours, Toni. You have the beast, and the man, but only when you are ready. But in the interest of being open and honest, I will share my plan with you. See, I'm gonna get you so addicted to me, you never want to leave."

"Keep this up, Pierce, and your plan is already working," she whispered, kissing his chest, and that tiny little move settled something inside of him.

He just had to keep to his plan, and that was all about the timing.

Chapter Ten

The afternoon wore away with Pierce and Toni frolicking in the lake, eating a little more, and making love again in the afternoon sunshine.

He still had her peaches and honey flavor on his lips from when he'd slid down her body and gave her the most intimate of kisses. Gods, he loved the way she'd cried out his name, body arching as he fucked her on his tongue, tasting her orgasm as it pulsed through her. She was the sexiest damn woman he had ever seen, and the wondrous thing was, she didn't even know it.

Her ex had done a number on her confidence, but Pierce hoped to remove that motherfucker's taint from her soul with patience and attention.

Each and every touch, kiss, climax, and surrender were victories in the war for Toni's freedom from her past. Pierce was over the fucking moon that he got to be the one to see her shine. And shine, she did. Like a fucking beacon calling to him alone.

After their lovemaking, they'd both fallen asleep in a tangle of arms and legs. Good thing Uncle Uzzi had bid the Neta close the cabins and lake for the weekend just for them. It was like the old Witch had known they would need this privacy, and he was glad.

His chest rumbled with a strange purring sound from his beast and Pierce frowned. That was new. New, but right. The animal could not get enough of her as he cuddled Toni on the blanket. The waning afternoon sun was warm and casting shadows from the leaves across her supple skin.

He took the opportunity to study her in slumber. He knew Shifters fell fast, especially when it was fated, but fuck. He did not know he was even capable of feeling so strongly about another person. She was it. She was all.

He was glad he woke before her and wished he could lie there with her draped across him all day. But mother nature had other plans for him. Pierce frowned and eased her body to the blanket, covering her with a towel before walking away to relieve himself by a tree with her still in his line of sight. They hadn't installed restrooms yet, though it was on their list of things to add to the area.

Good thing he hadn't gone far. The sound of snuffling and chuffing reached his ears, and he turned to see Toni's furry stalker not too far away from him.

"You have got to be kidding me," he grumbled, turning to the bear, and waving his arms around.

"Beat it! Get out of here," he whisper-growled.

The boxy-headed bastard snorted and peeled back his lips as if he were laughing at him. Fucking bear. The bear pawed at the ground, clearly having no intention of leaving, and Pierce growled louder.

"You know, you two are awfully cute like that."

Pierce jumped, spinning around to see an amused and completely bare-assed Toni standing with her arms crossed over her chest. His cock immediately stood at attention, the damn thing practically waving at her. Heart hammering in his chest, she grinned at him, and his mouth went dry.

What the hell had he been doing again?

Oh yeah.

He snorted and shook his head as the wild black bear chuffed and tried to walk past him to get to

Toni. Pierce reached out and shoved the big guy back. Was he kidding?

The bear grunted, walking a few steps away, but he turned back, baring his teeth at Pierce. Like he was annoyed the man was standing in his way. That woke the Tiger up, and Pierce flashed some fangs of his own. Toni really giggled then.

"Go on, Yogi, beat it. We're going home now, too," she told the creature who chuffed and watched her from further away, adoration in his beady black eyes.

Pierce's Tiger snarled louder.

"Hey, don't be mean. Yogi is a sweetheart," she cooed.

"Yogi is an adult black bear that likely weighs more than my Tiger," Pierce said, still kinda pissed about it.

"Yeah, well, I won't let him hurt you," Toni teased, wrapping her arms around Pierce's neck.

She pulled him down and he went willingly, loving the feel of her soft, smooth body against his. He kissed her deeply. Long, plucking, biting kisses that made her shiver in his arms.

"You know this is big, right?" he asked, pressing his forehead to hers.

"I know," she whispered.

"You okay with that, pretty girl? Because, fair warning, I've been known to dig in my heels when I want something."

She blinked up at him slowly, contentment on her pretty face. He noticed her black lashes were thick and short, and her eyes were glowing gold with her beast.

"You were pretty clear about that part before. But, uh, are you saying you want me, big guy?"

"I'm saying I want and plan on keeping you, pretty girl."

"No one ever wanted to keep me before. Well, except Stefan—"

Pierce's growl filled the air, and Toni pressed herself more firmly against him.

"Hey, I didn't say that to make you jealous," she blurted, and he cut off the sound.

"Shit, sorry, I know that. It's the Tiger. Wants to claim you," he growled, noting the shock in her eyes.

"But I won't Toni, not without your say so, okay? You have nothing to fear from me."

The Tiger was still there, in his voice. Pierce looked up, trying to get himself under control.

"I believe you, Pierce," she told him, cupping his face and forcing his gaze back to hers.

"I believe you and I trust you. And, well, I want to thank you for going slow with me."

"Skinny dipping and lake sex is slow? Damn girl, I hope I can keep up when you decide to move fast," he teased, catching her laughter with his kiss.

"Alright, enough. Take me home and feed me," she said when they came up for air. Pierce raised an eyebrow.

"Done. Let's go," he took her hand and pulled her to where they parked the ATV.

"Um, Pierce, maybe we can put our clothes on first and get our stuff?"

"Well, damn woman. You got me so mixed up," he chuckled, picking her up and spinning her around.

After a tickle fight, some splashing in the lake, and a little more making out, they finally got dressed and loaded the ATV. Pierce could not stop smiling the entire drive back to the cabin. The sun had dipped low, but he knew the area like the back of his hand, plus, the whole night vision thing came in handy at times like these.

He still could not believe how this whole thing was turning out. Toni was so much more than he'd ever dared dream. She was so much fun to be with. He loved teasing smiles from her and just letting her just talk. He got the feeling she was always a good listener, but maybe not someone people listened to very often. Like really listened to, as in being an ear for her to confide whatever feelings or issues she was dealing with.

Oh, he had no doubt she was a leader. She showed true leadership skills in the way she gave direction and was self-assured in certain things. But it was those tiny little hints of vulnerability that melted his heart. Toni was a strong Shifter, but she was human, too.

It was clear she loved her family and was a shoulder for her siblings or a kick in the ass, depending on what they needed. Loyalty was one helluva quality to recommend her to his heart, and she was already in there, roots growing steadily.

The whole mess at her job seemed fishy to him. His lawyer senses were tingling, but he would not interfere unless she okayed it. Toni just was not the kind of woman to make a deal without checking all the angles and doing her research. He already knew her better than that, and it surprised him her bosses didn't recognize that quality.

Clearly, *Eat Well Live Proud* was not the company he thought it was, if this was how they treated valuable employees. Still, he forced himself to let it go for now.

Toni looked happy, content. Maybe it was the sunshine. Or the somewhat forced vacation they'd both been told to take. Maybe it was kismet. Or maybe it was the smokin' hot smexy times they'd gotten up to. Hell, it could be all the above.

Whatever put that sweet, soft, tender smile on her pretty face, Pierce was down for more of it. Hell, he was down for all of it. Even his Tiger wanted to be there to see it. He wanted to be there to see her face bright and happy, wearing the smile he put there every single day of his life—if he was lucky.

Please let me be lucky.

Oh, she might not fully understand what she'd done, but Tonie Golden was his now. Marked or not, she was his and he was hers. Body, heart, and soul. She had the fealty of his beast. A seven hundred and fifty pound Tiger at her beck and call.

His body hummed with happiness as he turned down the lane that would take them back to the cabin. Of course, that was when he saw a bunch of cars in the driveway and his own face turned down in a scowl.

"That's her, officers, Antonetta Golden. Arrest her!"

What. The. Fuck.

Chapter Eleven

T oni was on cloud nine. She was deliciously sore, and so freaking happy she could burst. Pierce was one heck of a lover—*and that was putting it mildly.*

The man was a total sex god. For a Lioness who'd been categorized as off limits to her entire Pride for being any number of things, ranging from prudish to ice cold, it was something of a revelation.

He made her feel sexy, desired, wanted, and cared for. His aqua colored eyes had never left her, not once the whole time he was making love to her—*and yes, that was how it had felt.*

It was tender and empowering, soul shaking, truth be told. She supposed this was why Uncle Uzzi was so famous. He'd barely spoken to her before he set her up with the man of her dreams.

Magic works in mysterious ways, she supposed. But she was not questioning it. Toni was too damn happy to care how it worked. She turned her head to catch a glimpse of Pierce.

Gods, he was so handsome. Good looking in that way all Shifters had about them, he was more than that though. He wore his dark hair longer on top and shorn on the sides. It was thick, wavy, and glossy, like he used the good stuff to wash and condition it and did not care who knew.

His nose was strong, his teeth straight and white, thin lips that somehow turned into the most wicked grin she'd ever seen. He seemed to possess a chronic case of five o'clock shadow that made him look just disreputable enough to merit bad boy hotness.

And those eyes—gods, did she mention his eyes? Pure aquamarine that belonged on some male sea lord in a fairytale, or one of the dirty fantasy romances she loved to read.

Naughty boy. Sexy boy.

He was tall and well-muscled, the kind of physique obtained from working, not preening in a gym. She appreciated he knew the value of hard work, and the results were drool worthy. But he was not all brawn, the man had brains, too. And wasn't that something?

Matings were not always about love. Toni had learned that lesson when she was just a cub, over-hearing her mother and father go at it over the years. Oh, they'd tried to hide it from the kids. They were not bad people. Honestly, she loved her mom to bits. But her dad's leaving was the best thing to happen to any of them.

Toni was not going to borrow trouble now. Uncle Uzzi must have foreseen at least some of this when she'd finally asked for his help. So, no, matings did not always equal love. But if she were being honest, and she always tried to be, Toni was already there.

She was just about to say it, too, figuring she had nothing to lose and everything to gain by the confession. Only Toni did not have the chance. No sooner did Pierce

"That's her, officers, Antonetta Golden. Arrest her!"

Pierce's chest rumbled, a snarl threatening to escape his lips. She scented humans, instinctively placing her hands on him.

"Shh, normals," she whispered.

This was wrong. All wrong.

"Excuse me, miss? Can you please exit the vehicle?" an armed officer brandishing a Burlington County Sheriff's Department badge asked warily.

His partner, a smaller, slighter female officer, had her hand hovering just above her weapon, and Toni frowned. She smelled fear in the air, and it made her Lioness angsty.

"Mr. Bixby?" Toni gasped.

"Excuse me, Officer? My name is Pierce McDowd. I am the legal counsel for Maverick Development. You are trespassing on private property, and I must insist you leave without the proper court orders or a search warrant."

"Mr. McDowd, I'm Lieutenant Langley, this is Officer Duluth. Apologies for coming here without notice. We were not aware this was private property, and since the house was unlocked and the front door opened, we went inside and found this in the open," he said, indicating a plastic evidence bag with a laptop inside.

"That's my work laptop, but I left it in the office," Toni said, shock and confusion warring inside of her.

"Miss Golden, we found that computer sitting on the counter and with it sensitive information. You could be charged with corporate espionage—"

"I am sorry, this is ridiculous. You can't just barge in on private property and conduct a search—" Pierce interrupted, his anger palpable in the air.

"Excuse me, sir. But that is something you can argue in court. Right now, Miss Golden, you need to come with us," Officer Duluth said, opening a pair of handcuffs.

"Mr. Bixby? I left that laptop in your office. I didn't steal anything. I wouldn't!" Toni yelled, panic damn near crippling her.

"Toni! Toni, look at me," Pierce said, his deep voice strong, demanding her attention. "I am going to figure this out. Don't talk to anyone until I get there except to say you are invoking your right to counsel. Alright? Just stay calm, pretty girl. I got you, okay?"

Toni's gaze flicked to his glittering eyes. Pierce was holding on by a thread, and she knew instinctively what he was really asking of her. His Tiger was threatening to burst right out of him and shred these fuckers, and that would mess things up for everyone. All supernaturals would be outed, and keeping their secret was huge in their world.

"Okay," she said, nodding and wanting nothing more than to set him at ease.

Why the fuck did Bixby bring humans here?

Something was not right with that male, and she should have seen it a hundred times before today. His nasty little face was scrunched up like a rat's, and he watched her with raw hatred blazing in his eyes.

But why? What did she ever do to him? Shit. There would be time to figure it out later. Right now, she needed to calm down and get back in control. If not for herself, then for Pierce. If they were ever going to have a chance, they could not start with the murder of a couple of human law enforcement officers.

"Toni?" he growled, his whole body tense.

"I'm okay. I will be okay, I swear. Pierce, easy now," she whispered the last, waiting for him to really look at her.

Aquamarine eyes filled with turmoil met hers, and she could have cried for all the emotion she saw there. She pulled away from the officer, cupping Pierce's face, keeping his gaze on hers before she bared her soul to him.

"I love you," she said softly, without frills or any extras.

It was just *I love you*, plain and simple and true. What else did there need to be? That confession was for his ears only. Fuck Bixby and the two normals.

They could hang for all she cared. Uncle Uzzi

was right. Toni was deserving of something more than just working a thankless job for a boss who was out to get her for some unknown reason.

"Fuck. Here? You tell me you love me here, now? Dammit woman," he mumbled, then caught her lips in a hard, fast kiss. "I love you, too. So fucking much already. I'll have you out in no time," he promised.

Toni's heart squeezed inside her chest, and she tasted her own tears on her lips when they finally pulled apart at the lieutenant's insistence. Pierce's lips were drawn in a tight line. She watched him watching her, his whole body frozen, as the female officer cuffed Toni and guided her to one of the two Sheriff's Department cars sitting there.

The officer remained outside the vehicle, waiting until her boss told her to get in. They were stuck behind his car, so Toni was still able to follow the conversation. She listened, trying not to give in to the panic.

"Here's my card with the address where she will be interviewed—"

"You will not interview her until I arrive, and I will be right behind you," he said, but the last part was spoken to Toni, who could hear him fine through the glass.

"Fine. But since we have the evidence in hand, we

are going to arrest and charge her today. Mr. Bixby has already signed the complaint for the company."

"Toni, it will be okay. Just don't say a word without me. I'm grabbing my wallet and phone and I will be right behind you," he told her.

"You are charging her, right?" Bixby asked the lieutenant as the human male walked to the passenger's side of the car and held the door opened for the man.

Smart of him to get a ride, Toni thought, If he were paying attention, he would have seen the danger lurking behind him in Pierce's Tiger bright eyes. The moron didn't seem to realize he was the hunted one now.

She watched Pierce for as long as she could see him, his aquamarine gaze glittering in the early evening haze. She turned her body, trying to keep him in sight as they rounded a bend, but then, poof, he was gone.

Toni closed her eyes and bit her bottom lip. This was all wrong. She replayed her last day in Bixby's office. He'd instructed her to leave her work computer there, and she did, only taking some personal effects from her desk.

"Excuse me. Was there a warrant?" Toni asked, completely flummoxed by the whole thing.

"Didn't your lawyer tell you to be quiet?" the officer retorted.

The nasty woman was right, but something was really bothering Toni. Like where the hell were they taking her? The cabin was located in Burlington County, but the Eat Well Live Proud offices were in Maccon County. This made no sense.

"Where are we going?" she asked, trying to figure out the direction.

"Oh, just to processing," Officer Snarky Pants said.

"But we're going the wrong way. The lieutenant gave Pierce his card, and I am pretty damn sure this is not how you get to the Burlington County Sheriff's department," she said, mildly panicked.

Toni was meticulous about details, especially when it came to driving places she had never been. So, before setting out to Mount Maverick, she'd googled the directions, checking all the relevant points, including the location of the local police and sheriff's department.

Call it a quirk, but just in case Uncle Uzzi set her up with a serial killer, Toni had wanted to know where to run. When they reached the end of the mountain road, Officer Duluth should have stayed on the highway, headed west. But she didn't. Duluth got off, circled back east, and started taking back roads. Now Toni was all mixed up.

"It was a good performance, wasn't it? Now, why don't you go to sleep," the woman, clearly not an officer, said, placing a gas mask on her face just as a sour smelling mist filled the back of the police car.

Toni's eyes went wide. She slammed on the windows with her fists, but the handcuffs didn't give her much leverage, and the windows must have been reinforced or something. She started to feel dizzy.

Shit. Now what?

Her eyes burned, and she closed them, sinking to her knees on the floor of the cruiser. Maybe if she got low enough, the mist wouldn't get into her lungs. Toni tried to call on her beast for strength, but her Lioness went silent.

Panic gripped her then. Even as she tried to take shallow breaths, the gas was already working. Her eyes and body grew heavy, and Toni slumped forward, her face against the old car mat. The last thing she saw was an old bloodstain with some clumps of hair still sticking to it, but her thoughts were on Pierce.

Only Pierce.

Chapter Twelve

"What do you mean, she is not here?" Pierce asked.

The male normal, who was acting desk sergeant at the Burlington County Sheriff's Department, rolled his eyes before turning back to Pierce. He looked bored, and frankly, uninterested. Neither of which gave Pierce any confidence the man knew what he was doing.

"Sir, like I have said ten times already, no one with the name Antonetta Golden, or matching her description, has come through these doors today."

"This is insanity. Where is Lieutenant Langley? I need to see him. She was in Officer Duluth's car."

"Who? There is no Lieutenant Langley or Officer Duluth here, sir. Is this a prank? I warn you there are serious consequences for wasting the time of law enforcement," the man retorted, shaking his head as he went back to sorting the mail.

Thunder roared in Pierce's ears. What the fuck was going on? He needed answers, and he needed them now. But before he could reach across the desk and shake the unhelpful human, Hunter came bursting through the doors, Uncle Uzzi in tow.

"Pierce," he called his name, and the Tiger obeyed, forcing his feet to move.

"Any news?" Uncle Uzzi asked.

He had called both from his car after the two Sheriff's Department vehicles left with Toni in tow. Pierce had run inside to grab his keys, wallet, and phone before jumping in his Jeep and trailing after them. He hadn't even bothered to dress, which had caused some friction when he arrived since he'd been shirtless and shoeless in a bathing suit.

Thank fuck, like most Shifters, he had extra clothes in his trunk and went to put them on before returning. Clad in jeans, a t-shirt, and sneakers, he paced the floor. Anger and fear rolled through him as he spoke to Hunter and Uncle Uzzi.

"No. They don't have her. It seems there is no Lieutenant Langley or Officer Duluth. Fuck, I could not have been more than five minutes behind them!

There was an accident on the highway, and I got stuck behind it. Nevertheless, they should have been here if they were fucking real," he growled, earning him some strange stares from the humans afoot.

Shit.

He covered his face with his hands and agreed to moving their conversation back to the Pride House. They would not get any answers from the normals. He'd sniffed the air inside.

Toni never stepped foot inside there. There was absolutely no trace of her peaches and honey scent anywhere. In fact, he did not get a single hint of any Lioness at all.

She was gone.

Something froze in Pierce at that terrifying thought. Toni was gone. She'd been taken. But by whom?

Fuck. He hadn't even realized Hunter and Uzzi had herded him into their car until they arrived back at the Pride House. Elissa, the Nari of the Maverick Pride, was standing on the wraparound porch, her swollen belly outlined in her swing dress, her cubs, Melly and Celia playing at her feet.

"Did you find her?" she asked, worry creasing her brow.

"No, my love. But we will," Hunter said, kissing her sweetly, and bending down to lift his girls.

Normally the scene would warm something inside of Pierce, but not then. His mate was missing, and he did not know how to find her. Shit. He'd fucked up badly. What was happening to her? Where was she?

Rage at his own impotence filled him, and he cursed and paced, pulling on his hair as he held his head.

"Fuuuucccccckkkk!" he roared, falling to his knees as two more cars pulled up.

"Pierce!" Uncle Uzzi walked over to him. "Come, this is not helping her," the old man said, and yes, he was right.

People spilled out of the newly arrived cars, one held the King and Queen of the Blue Valley Pride. The Lioness was an older version of Toni, and Pierce introduced himself and explained what he knew.

By the time he was finished, all of her sisters were there, two of them with their mates, and Toni's mother looked ready to kill someone. He felt about two inches tall. But he didn't blame them for his shortcomings.

What the fuck had happened?

"I did not notice anything wrong with the two

officers. Toni was upset, but I needed her calm. I was fighting my change. There were humans. She trusted me to get her out. I failed her," he growled, tears pricking his eyes.

"No, son. You did right. You could not have known," the King said magnanimously.

"Where is my sugar cub? Where did they bring her?" Patricia Golden-Crowley asked, emotion making her voice vibrate.

"Easy, love. We will find her," King Donovan, Primus of the Blue Valley Lion Pride, murmured and put his arm around his mate.

"Let's go over it again. When and how did this all happen?"

"I messed up. We had spent a wonderful afternoon together, I was so happy. She was, too. Then, when we got back to the cabin, they were waiting. They had proof she'd stolen a laptop. Fuck, the whole search was illegal. I should never have let them take her," Pierce replied, more than willing to accept the blame.

His chest squeezed him. The beast inside raking his claws over his soul, shredding him. Pierce felt as though he were suffocating.

"No, no one is saying that," Hunter said, joining them. "Look, Pierce, you did the right thing, the only thing you could have. If you would have shifted, fought humans, I would be calling the Shifter Council on you right now," Hunter told him, clapping a hand on his back.

"Pierce, back up a second," Uncle Uzzi said, dragging his attention down to the older Witch.

"Yes, Uncle Uzzi?" he asked, shoulders tense.

"You said there was no way that laptop was there beforehand, correct?" the older male asked.

"Wait, I mean, Toni is a workaholic. She might have snuck one on her vacation," Annabeth, one of her sisters, inserted.

"No, she wouldn't. You weren't there Annabeth. Toni was really upset the day her new boss told her to go home and specifically mentioned him telling her not to take the computer," Adrianna, another sister, added.

"That's right," their mother said, turning to Pierce. "Did you see her with a computer during your little rendezvous, hot stuff?"

"Hey," growled the King, glaring at his mate.

"What? My sugar cub is a looker, makes sense she would match up with one, right Uncle Uzzi?"

"I am not quite certain that is how it works, Patricia. But yes, I agree she is very lovely, as are all your daughters. Now, Pierce?" Uncle Uzzi replied, getting them back on track.

"Oh, uh, no, she didn't have a computer. In fact, she barely used her phone," Pierce said.

"Wait. I know! What about you?" Elissa asked. "Can't you track her through your matebond?"

"No," Pierce replied, teeth clenched. "I didn't claim her—"

"I take it back, you're no hot stuff, you're an idiot!" shouted Patricia, ramming her painted claw into his chest.

Pierce winced, but he would never raise his hand to a female, much less the mother of the woman he intended to take as mate. All three Golden sisters bared their fangs, giving him dirty looks, but he shook his head.

"Ladies, please. I love your sister and have every intention of claiming her, but she will decide when she is ready. Not me or you or anyone else," he replied with muted power lacing his voice.

There were things Pierce would always be willing to bend on. But this was not one of them. Toni was quite capable of making her own decisions, and it was time everybody recognized that fact.

"You love her? It's been like a second," Adrianna scoffed.

"Well, to be truthful, Adrianna, I fell in love with Toni in far less time than a second. More like a moment, then boom, lightning, thunder, universes exploded into existence, and I loved her," he said, truth ringing in his voice.

"But you still didn't claim her," Adrianna stated, as if that said everything.

"Look, Toni is not the kind of woman who needs a man browbeating her into accepting his claim. I promised I would wait until she was comfortable and ready, and I will. But that is none of anyone's business but ours," he growled.

"I take it back. You really are perfect for my sugar cub, hot stuff," Patricia said, grinning like the devil.

The older Lioness' face sobered, and Pierce knew what she was feeling because he was feeling it, too. The fact Toni was gone, missing, kidnapped hit him harder than a ton of bricks.

"I promise I won't stop looking. I can't. I refuse to lose her," Pierce vowed.

"Okay, so we know the laptop was planted," Uncle Uzzi said, getting them back on track. "What else do we know?"

"Toni devoted lots of time to work," Annabeth said.

"Yeah, she was promoted to a new department

last year, and given her own campaign to run, which was like a huge deal," Adrianna added.

"Is that usual? To give an expensive marketing campaign to someone new to the department?" Pierce asked.

"Um, no," Ariella spoke up. "It is not usual, but we never questioned it. Toni is great at whatever she does,"

"Yes, she is," Pierce said, a tight smile on his face, "King Donovan, excuse me? But who runs EWLP?" Pierce asked, going full on lawyer mode.

There were pieces to this puzzle missing, and he needed more information if he was going to get to the bottom of this.

"You mean am I a figurehead incapable of running the day-to-day operations?" the man growled.

"Oh, well, no, sir. I am simply assuming you are busy with the Pride," Pierce said, trying not to offend the powerful Primus.

"Ha ha! You should see your face, dear boy. You assumed correctly. Maggie Pierce has recently been promoted to CEO of Eat Well Live Proud. Matthew Periwinkle, an old friend, has taken her job as regional manager, and let me see. Hmm. I am afraid that is all I can recall offhand."

"What about a Mr. Bixby? He was the male who came to the cabin with the imposters."

Another car arrived to join their party, and Leo Crowley, King Donovan's son, and a detective with the Blue Valley PD, exited the vehicle along with his mate, Sheila Rand. Concerned expressions on their faces, they were greeted by the other Lions. The couple stopped and said hello to Hunter, Elissa, and the other Maverick Pride Tigers, as well, but Pierce did not care about formalities. He needed info.

"Have you found out anything more about Toni?" Pierce asked, desperate for any hint of news.

"I'm sorry. No, we have not. Annabeth filled me in on the way over. Tell me, did you see any badges on the two officer impersonators?" the Lion asked, no nonsense while his mate comforted Toni's mother and weepy sisters.

"Yeah, of course. They had badges, official vehicles, everything but a warrant. The bastards," Pierce growled. "I was asking your father about the changes to personnel at EWLP. Do you know a guy named Bixby?"

"Bixby? Marion Bixby?" Leo asked, head canted to the side.

Electricity charged the air, and Pierce froze. Dread filled him, and his gut twisted. Why was Leo's face contorted into a mask of horror at that name? He did not want to think bad thoughts, but right then, he imagined the worst.

Whoever the fuck Marion Bixby really was, Pierce was going to tear him a new asshole if he so much as touched a hair on Toni's sweet head.

Grrrr.

Chapter Thirteen

"I believe so, yes," Pierce said, trying to recall.

"Motherfucker," Leo growled. "Marion Bixby is a known alias for Tom Perry. That Lion is a disgrace. His rap sheet is a mile long petty theft, burglary, forgery, fraud. What does he have to do with this?"

"Marion Bixby is Toni's boss," Adrianna added.

"He's the bastard who brought the humans to Pride lands to have Toni arrested," Pierce growled.

"I thought Maggie was her boss," Leo returned, talking over Adrianna.

"No, she got promoted, remember?" Adrianna told Leo.

Her golden eyes were so similar to her sister's it hurt Pierce to look at her.

Fuck. Toni. Toni. Where are you?

Pierce's Tiger was roaring inside him. He tried to locate any hint of a matebond, but it was too faint without them performing the whole ritual of biting and marking each other. He could have screamed his frustration, but who would that help?

This was not a time to be selfish. Toni needed him. He turned to look at Adrianna, who was shaking his arm. Her eyes were wide open, and it looked like she was on the verge of putting two and two together.

"What is it Ade?" Pierce asked.

"Leo, you said Perry. Tom Perry, right?" Adrianna asked, licking her lips nervously.

"Yeah, I did, why?" the big Lion asked, walking over to the two of them.

"Ade? Do you know something?" Pierce asked, taking her by the shoulders.

"There was a managerial overhaul when Ms. Pierce became CEO. All new people, some department changes. If Bixby's name really is Perry, then this is starting to make sense," Adrianna muttered.

"Here, let me pull up the file I have on him and his known associates," Leo grunted. The Lion pulled a Toughbook out of his briefcase.

"This is Pride, not police issued. I've got records

of all known supernatural offenders and anyone they work with. This database is still in its early stages, but supernatural agencies are starting to share information, and with the help of Graves Enterprises and Draco Fortis software developments, we are on the cusp of cooperation the likes of which the supernatural world has never seen," Leo explained and started pulling up files.

"That's very interesting," Adrianna said, eyes wide.

"Found him! Seems he works scams with a relative, a nephew," Leo growled when he found Bixby's file. Pierce leaned over the guy's shoulder, speed reading the page.

"Shit. That's what I thought," Adrianna whispered, and her face fell.

"Motherfucker. His nephew's name is Stefan?" Pierce asked, his beast clawing the shit out of him.

"Yep, all those crimes I mentioned before, but it seems he recently moved up to embezzlement and corporate espionage. This fucker is a real piece of work. Yeah, Stefan Perry is his nephew, and one of his known associates. The guy has his own rap sheet, including assault and battery on a few exes. Why?"

"I'm going to hunt that motherfucker if he

touches one hair on her head," Pierce snarled, fighting to control his Tiger.

"What the hell is going on?" Leo asked.

"Stefan Perry is Toni's ex-boyfriend. They dated about a year ago, but he's been harassing her nonstop. He is a real piece of shit," Adrianna supplied.

"What the fuck? This guy was still bothering Toni?"

"Yeah, I haven't even told her about the deliveries of dead roses, rotten meat, torn up pictures of her," Adrianna murmured.

"Ade, why would you hide that?" Annabeth asked, rubbing her protruding belly with tears swimming in her eyes.

"Easy, baby," Hank said to her and held his mate while she cried.

"Because she was finally going out again. And she agreed to talk to Uncle Uzzi. Look, I am sorry, I didn't know he would do this. I just, you guys, you didn't see how hard it was on her being with that guy. He took the light right out of her eyes, and I couldn't let him get his hooks in her again," Adrianna stated, shoulders shaking as she sobbed.

"Okay, I just texted some buddies, they are searching for Stefan now. So let me run through this," Leo said. "First, Toni gets promoted to a new department and is given a huge opportunity. Second, there is some discrepancy over the job she did, and she gets suspended by her boss, Marion Bixby, aka Tom Perry. Third, she gets arrested."

"Yeah, but this whole thing where he accused her of being negligent with the ad campaign is bullshit. Toni would never do a shoddy job," Ariella chirped in.

"I don't doubt that," Leo said. "But we are missing something."

"Let's find that fucker, force him to shift, and wax all the fur from his stupid body," Ariella, one of the pregnant Golden girls, growled angrily.

"Good idea, Ari, but one minute, okay? Lemme get this straight." Sheila, Leo's mate, began pacing as she spoke.

"That pussy Stefan tried to bully our girl into mating him, playing on her insecurities, being a dick, and when she said no, he waited to exact his revenge by having his uncle make her look incompetent at best and criminal at worst?"

"No," Pierce said, joining the discussion. "He is taking his revenge by kidnapping her and forcing her to take his bite. We know he is abusive. We know he has beaten women, one who later died of her wounds. Those women were human. Toni is different. She is a challenge. She is a Shifter like him, so she can take more. He wants to hurt her," growled Pierce.

"Not if we hurt him first," Adrianna snarled.

Pierce looked at her and nodded. He was totally on board with that. All he knew was he needed to find his mate. Now.

"Brother, anything you need, we are here for you," Hunter told him.

Having the support of his Neta and his Pride, the Lions too, made all the difference. Pierce nodded, and they got to work. Tracking that soon-to-be-dead asshole was not easy, but Pierce had every confidence they would be successful.

There was literally no other option. Everyone there was either on the phone or on their laptop, emailing and calling contacts across the Garden State.

"What does he want? Revenge? Money? That POS! He better not hurt one hair on my sugar cub!" Patricia wailed.

"How the hell did Marion Bixby get a job at EWLP? Dad?" Leo turned to his father.

The two Lion males shook their heads, each on the phone with assistants and special ops people.

Pierce felt fucking powerless, and he hated it. Standing at the corner of the Pride House, Pierce crossed his arms and looked into the woods. That was odd. He thought he saw something peering at him through the leaves.

"Yes? Ah ha! Good," Uncle Uzzi walked over and tapped him on the shoulder. "Yes. Where is he? Great. We will see you in a few minutes," the man said.

"Uncle Uzzi, what is it? Did something happen?" Pierce asked, his attention on the older male.

"Contacts in Barvale have discovered our Mr. Bixby and are now detaining him," he said, mouth turned down in a moue of distaste. "They are bringing in someone to interview him."

"Interview him?" Adrianna asked.

"It is better you do not know," Uncle Uzzi replied gently, though his face was hard as stone.

The minutes ticked by slowly, and Pierce felt as though he was losing his mind. He walked to the end of the property, hands on top of his head, hissing a slow breath. There it was again. The sound of something just beyond the stand of trees that signaled the start of the forest. That land stretched for a few miles, leading up to the base of Mount Maverick.

It was wild, thick, beautiful land, owned by the

Pride for over a century now. As Neta, Hunter was the caretaker of that sacred place, and his Tigers, like Pierce, took it upon them to keep it safe and protected. It added insult to injury that Toni was taken from him on their lands. Pierce's head was flooded with emotions.

Anger, fear, and blind fury the strongest among them. He needed her back.

"Yogi?" Pierce whispered, shocked at the giant black bear who lumbered slowly towards him.

The animal grunted and growled, head low as he pressed it into Pierce's side. Silly beast was probably looking for Toni. Had he walked this far just to find the Shifter he was smitten with? Pierce closed his eyes and reached out, petting the animal.

"I want her, too, buddy. Wait. What the?"

Pierce's eyes flashed as he took his hand away from the bear's matted fur. It was sticky and warm, wet with something. He sniffed. Shit. Blood. The big animal collapsed, moaning softly, his breathing labored, and Pierce yelled for help.

"Fuck. Oh fuck, Come on Yogi," he growled.

"What is it?"

"Get Mikey! The bear's been mauled. Fuck, shit, no Yogi, hold on," he cried out.

Leo, Uncle Uzzi, and the rest of them joined him,

racing to where Pierce was leaning over the bear. He ripped off his shirt and pressed it against one of the animal's wounds.

"What bear?" Hunter asked, running to see the problem.

"This bear. He's been attacked, mauled. We need to help him!"

"I've called Mikey," Elissa said, jogging next to them. "But Pierce, what does this have to do—"

"This bear is in love with Toni. First time I saw her she was wrestling the thing for a bag of cookies," he said, a ghost of a grin on his face.

"Yep, that sounds like Toni," Adrianna sniffed, ripping the bottom of her shirt, and holding it on another of the bear's injuries.

"Gods, he's been ripped up," Ariella murmured.

"He's a brave old guy, aren't you, Yogi?" Pierce said.

He leaned down, sniffing the bear's fur. It wasn't just the bear's blood he scented. There was Lion blood mixed in and beyond that, the smell of peaches and honey.

Toni.

Pierce knew beyond a doubt the bear had found Toni, and he'd tried to protect her. Uncle Uzzi's phone rang, and while the man took it, Pierce made up his mind. All in, he was all in when it came to Toni.

"You are a courageous, bold, total badass, woman," Pierce grunted and kissed the moaning animal's head.

"Pierce?" Hunter asked as Mikey came running with supplies.

"What's happened?" the Pride healer asked.

"Smell that?" Pierce asked Hunter, his gaze flicking to Leo's.

"That's Lion blood," the detective growled.

"Yep. Male Lion. This bear is a hero. He's been brawling with the motherfucker who stole Toni. Now, I'm gonna follow his trail back to her," Pierce told them.

"Bixby just confessed to the Barvale Clan Enforcer. He and his nephew set Toni up for a fall. He was supposed to take her from her house, but she wasn't there, so he hired two human mercenaries to act as officers and arrest her. Their job was to bring her to Stefan, but Bixby doesn't know where they were meeting."

"It would have to be close," Leo said, nodding at the bear.

"Pierce?" Adrianna called. "Where are you going?"

"I'm gonna go hunt down that sonofabitch and I'm gonna bring my mate home," he growled, tearing off his clothes as he headed to the tree line.

"Not alone, you're not," she muttered as Pierce's Tiger ripped out of him.

The sounds of the others shifting reached his ears, but he was already on the move. The bear's scent was fresh in the air, all he had to do was follow the trail.

Hold on, pretty girl. I'm coming for you.

Chapter Fourteen

T oni moaned. Her head was pounding like she'd been drinking catnip-laced tequila nonstop for days, and her throat was raw as fuck. She coughed, wheezing as someone pushed her upright.

"There she is," a voice whispered.

She felt hands brushing her hair back and felt a hard male body beneath her. Toni tried to open her eyes to see who was whispering and touching her so familiarly. Her skin was crawling, and she felt like she was going to hurl.

"Come on, kitten. Open those big eyes for me," the voice growled. "I'm gonna make it all okay now."

"Stefan?" she moaned, scrambling off him.

Her body felt wrong. Heavy and uncoordinated.

She backed up against a wall, whimpering when she heard his footsteps nearing her. Toni rubbed at her face, trying to get the gunk out of her eyes.

"What happened? Where am I?"

"You're right where you belong, kitten. I forgive you for everything. Don't worry. It will be good now," the voice said, and she remembered who it belonged to. Stefan. That was Stefan talking.

But what was he talking about? Her eyes hurt so badly, it was like she'd been hit with tear gas or something. Toni felt foggy and mixed up. She shivered and her stomach squeezed.

Ugh.

Shifters did not generally get sick. It was unusual, but it could happen. Still, why was she sick?

Questions filled her, and she shook her head and blinked, trying to focus, but the whole world was dark and blurry. How did she get here with Stefan? Where was here, anyway? Then she remembered.

She did not go anywhere with Stefan. Her traitorous ex had done something bad. Slowly, he came into focus, crouched in front of her, grinning like the cat that got the canary. Wait. She left him. They weren't dating anymore. Pierce. Where was Pierce?

Dread filled her as her vision cleared. Stefan was butt-naked, his penis erect, and he was staring at her like she was his dream come true. Glancing down, Toni saw she was naked, too.

Oh, no. No. NO. NO!

Bile filled her mouth, and before she could stop herself, she puked. Right on his feet. She scrubbed her hands over her body, trying to get his scent off her. She felt no soreness or anything, so she was not raped, but fuck, this was a violation. Anger filled her as he roared in revulsion at her sick that covered his feet.

"You fucking bitch!" he bellowed.

Stefan reared back, then lashed out with a claw-tipped hand and slapped her hard across the face. Blood dripped down her cheek, and Toni turned back to him and snarled.

Ooh, guess he did not like her puking on him. Well, good. That made the two of them. She did not like him anywhere near her. Fucking kidnapping prick. But even thinking the worst of him, she never expected him to have her arrested by fake cops and drugged. Wait. This went further than that. Bixby worked for him, too.

"What the hell are you doing, Stefan?"

"I am trying to give you a second chance, you ungrateful whore," he growled, standing up and grabbing some cloth to wipe his feet.

Toni looked around. They were in the woods somewhere, in a tent—*so gross*. There was a small lantern hanging on one of the tent poles, and a few bags and a cooler.

"A second chance? Are you delusional? We are broken up, I don't want a chance with you!" she hissed, grabbing a blanket from the pallet he'd made on the forest floor and covering her body.

"You have been ignoring my gifts, kitten," he growled and when he faced her again, she saw madness in his eyes, and a dagger in his hands.

"What are you talking about?"

"I sent you all your favorites. Flowers, chocolates, then when you ignored me, I sent you dead flowers, rotten meat to remind you to be grateful for my attention," he snarled.

Toni frowned. She never received anything from him. If she had, she would have taken it right to her cousin Leo, the detective. Toni gasped and closed her eyes.

Ade.

Her protective sister would have taken his offerings and tossed them in the trash to protect her. She was lucky to have sisters like that, sisters who wanted to protect and shield. Toni only hoped she would have the chance to tell her so.

Fuck that.

Of course, she would see Adrianna again. All her sisters. Her family. And Pierce. Yes, her mate, who she was going to claim as soon as she fucking got out of here. Toni was not going down without a fight. That was a fact, as the sting of her wounded cheek reminded her.

"I want nothing from you, Stefan. Especially not you," she enunciated each syllable, bracing herself for the attack she knew was coming.

"You don't mean that, kitten. Now, I smelled that bastard all over you, but I am willing to forget it. He's not a Lion, Toni. He can't give you the young I can. I was waiting for you to wake before I took you and bit you, but maybe you aren't worthy of that yet. I'll just knock you out again and when you wake, it will be too late."

"You're out of your mind," she growled, moving out of the way as he lunged for her.

"After a few months locked up out here with me," he growled, arms wide, preparing for his next attack. "You will see how lucky you are to have me to provide for you. See, Toni, you always thought you were better than me."

"That's not true, Stefan. I don't think I am better than anyone. I just don't like you," she retorted.

Toni was still wobbly on her feet. The drug did something to her Lioness, and until it got completely out of her system, the animal simply could not come forward. She backed up against the wall of the tent. Inching her way around it, trying to stay out of his way. If she could just reach the flap, maybe she could run away and get help.

"See kitten, you never understood me or my interest in you. You and me, we are the same. We will continue our kind. Purebred Shifters are so rare. So valuable on the black market. Did you know big game hunters would pay tens of thousands to hunt a purebred Lion Shifter?" he said and grinned evilly.

"You want to sell our cubs to be hunted?" she asked, horrified by the depths of his madness.

"Why not? We'll have plenty. Female with good hips can bear young for decades," he grunted and grunted before lunging to attack again.

Toni screamed, falling backwards out of the flap just as Stefan reached her. She cried out, expecting the dagger to have already pierced her flesh—*and really, what kind of small-dick-having-pussy brings a knife to a Shifter fight?*

But it never found purchase. Toni gasped, rolling out of the way. She got tangled in the blanket and tore it off her body as she struggled to stand up. Her eyes went wide as something big and brown and furry vaulted over her, its jaws wrapping around Stefan's wrist.

"Yogi!" she shouted in horror as the bear continued to bite down on Stefan's arm.

It was the one that held the knife, and the bear's eyes gleamed with rage as he shook, growling so loudly it was deafening. Stupid brave bear would have been successful had Stefan been merely a man. But he was a Lion Shifter, and even as the bear savaged his wrist, severing one hand from his body, the male had semi-shifted.

Toni screamed as Stefan raked his razor-sharp claws across the bear's hide, ripping open his shoulder. She attacked him then, using the element of surprise and her body weight to hit him sideways off the wild animal she'd come to care for so very much. Stefan struck her again, ripping a gash along her forearm, before he crawled away clutching his bleeding stump.

"Go on, Yogi! Get help! Get Pierce! Beat it, go!" Toni shouted, pointing to the woods before turning back to face her attacker.

"You bitch. Fucking bear. I will hunt you down, you dumb beast. Help me, cunt. Dammit, help me!"

Stefan screamed, but Toni shook her head, backing away from the crazed, bleeding male.

It was dark, and she had no idea where she was. But Stefan was hurt now, and that would slow him considerably. If she had any shot of surviving him, she had to start moving. Now.

Her face hurt from when Stefan hit her the first time. Toni could not bring herself to look down at the gory injury on her leg. The *pat pat pat* of blood dripping as it hit the forest floor was loud in her ears. Almost as loud as her breathing.

Though she hated to admit it, Toni was scared. Her inner Lioness was still unreachable. Whatever drug those assholes had used, it rendered her animal dormant. She only hoped it was temporary.

Minutes passed as she tried to gain some distance between her and the monster who'd taken her. However many, she didn't know. An owl screeched overhead, and she startled.

"I hate the woods," she muttered, trying to run on her bum leg, and failing.

Her voice was shaky, whether from adrenaline or cold, she didn't know. A deep rumbling growl sounded behind her, and Toni froze. The moon was full. Its light shone down between the branches and leaves of the forest's canopy, and she shivered as a giant male Lion ambled slowly forward.

He was missing his front paw, but that did not matter. He was not rushing her. The crazed look in his eyes told her he was too far gone to the beast. Whatever humanity Stefan had possessed was long gone now. He was all Lion, and she was his prey.

"Fuck," she mumbled, backing up against a tree.

Stefan the lame Lion snarled, his jaws dripping saliva. Toni winced, then straightened her spine. She was not ready to die like this. This bastard was not about to render her powerless.

An image of Pierce, that fierce, nurturing, protective male, ran through her mind, and she suddenly found her backbone. He believed in her. Said he would be there cheering her on, and she was damn well going to give him the chance.

"Come on, kitty," she growled to herself, calling her Lioness up from the drug-induced fog she was suffering. "Come on."

The big, angry male roared, the predatory sound echoing through the trees. Good. She hoped someone had heard it. Hoped they would send help. Toni knew they were on Maverick Pride lands. She'd smelled the scents of fur and Tiger for a while now.

Arrogant prick Stefan was, he'd overlooked that deadly fact.

Finally, she felt her Lioness stir just as Stefan sprinted on his one stump and three good legs. Dammit. Toni was too late. She closed her eyes, wanting the vision of her mate to be the last thing she saw, not this mangy murderous motherfucker.

I am so sorry, Pierce.

Chapter Fifteen

T he sound of impact nearly shattered her eardrums, but it was odd. Toni felt nothing. She opened her eyes and gasped as two snarling Cats savaged each other. Oh, it was brutal. The Tiger male was fueled by fury and vengeance, his hits just kept on coming and the crazed Lion did not stand a chance.

"Pierce," she gasped as he delivered the killing blow.

Tears of relief and joy spilled down her cheeks as she waited for him to turn to face her. His beast's growl reverberated through the woods as blood dripped from his fur. He bumped her with his head, sniffing and checking her for injury. The animal lapped at the gash on her leg, using his healing properties to help speed the repairs her Lioness was only now able to begin.

The Tiger paid the same attention to the scratches on her face. His sandpapery tongue felt good against her skin, and she moaned, running her hands over his fur, whispering words of thanks, love, and who knew what as she sagged against him.

The sound of others joining them reached her ears, but she didn't turn around. Pierce's fur receded and soon she was swept up in his steel arms. His breath mixed with hers as he kissed her, tears running unashamedly down his face.

"Fuck. I'm sorry. I am so sorry. I should have never let them take you—"

"Shh. It's okay. You came for me," she responded, kissing him back.

"I will always come for you," he swore. "Love you so much. Fuck, Toni, I would die without you. Can't live in this world if you aren't in it, pretty girl," he whispered, kissing her again.

The others stayed back, giving them space. She heard them moving, likely checking on that dead bastard. But she could not give a rat's ass about Stefan. She only wanted Pierce. Her mate.

Mine, the Lioness purred and Toni grinned, trusting her animal's choice now completely.

She clung tightly to Pierce, giving him everything she had with her kiss. She knew he'd been telling her the truth about his feelings. She could hear it in his words, just as she felt it in her heart.

"I love you," he said, and she nodded, repeating the words. "Gods, I was so scared when I heard his kill roar. I did not think I would get to you in time, Toni."

"I know. I am sorry—"

"No! You have nothing to be sorry for, you brave, beautiful badass. Damn woman, I never been so proud of anyone. You stood up to him."

"I did," she whispered, shivering at that fact.

"Yes, you did. You were still in your human skin, facing off with that insane fuck. Brave, brave mate," he said, and his eyes went wide.

"Why do you have that look on your face?" she asked, confused.

"Well, I called you mate, Toni, and I know how you feel about that. Shit. I'm sorry, it was insensitive, but don't be pissed, okay?"

"I couldn't be pissed at you if I tried," she replied, laughter and tears making her voice thick.

"Thank the gods," he murmured, kissing her forehead, then meeting her eyes again.

"What is it, Pierce? Tell me."

"Toni, I want to claim you. I know, I said I would wait for you, and I will, I swear I'll never break my promise or forget my vow to you. But I need you to know *you* are it for me. My Tiger picks you. I pick you. I'll wait, but you need to know how I feel. You are the love of my life. My mate," he growled, his voice thick with his Tiger, aqua eyes blazing with his beast.

She had never seen him more fierce or beautiful, covered in the remnants of his battle to rescue and avenge her. Yeah, she had tried to save herself. She would have failed, but he still acknowledged it as a triumph. He even praised the gods for getting him there in time.

Humble, humble man, taking no credit for his role in saving her life. He just held her, kissing her, praising her, loving her. And giving it all with no expectations of a return on his investments.

After a few more minutes of their sweet and poignant reunion, Pierce accepted a blanket from someone and wrapped it around Toni. Shifters were used to nudity, but after she explained everything that went down, she felt better having something to cover her. Pierce looked so angry when she told him about Stefan's plans, she would not have put it past the male to try to kill him all over again.

"It's okay. I'm okay," she told him, nodding at him to take the first pair of sweats one of their crew had brought.

"You should take them—" he tried, but she shook her head. She had already taken the sweatshirt and with the blanket tied around her waist, she was more than okay.

"I am so sorry, Toni," Pierce whispered, tucking her into his side after he slid the pants on.

Oh, she went willingly. The big, protective male could not seem to stop touching her, and she was fine with it. Truth was, Toni couldn't get enough of his touch either.

Leo had called the DPCA, the acronym stood for Department of Paranormal Creatures and Activity. It was a secret human and Shifter government agency that dealt with supernatural crimes and events like this one.

They cleaned the mess, got rid of Stefan's body, the tent, everything the maniac had brought with him. She'd had to go over it again, and that was fine. She was fine as long as she had Pierce to stand beside her.

"We found Officer Duluth's body, dead in the stolen Sheriff's Department car. It seems the suspect, Stefan Perry, killed her after she delivered you to him," Agent Margo Wells told her, and there was something familiar about the woman.

"I'm sorry. Do I know you?" Toni asked.

"Actually, yes, Miss Golden. I met you at my brother's clinic. You know him as Dr. Logan Wells," she replied with a grin. "I am mated to Egros Pyke, he developed the heat suppressant with Logan."

"Oh, I see. Well, tell them both thank you for me. Having control over my heat cycle means everything to me. Their work has been a real game changer for female Shifters," Toni said.

"I will tell them, Miss Golden, thanks."

"What about the man pretending to be the lieutenant?" Pierce asked.

"Yes, I am sorry, but he is still at large. We will keep you updated," Agent Wells said before leaving.

Pierce thanked the agent, speaking to some of his Pride before taking a cell phone. He said the name Mikey, but she had yet to meet all his Pride. She waited for him to finish the call, then waited as a look of relief crossed his face before he spoke.

"I did not mention this yet, but you should know, I found you because of Yogi," he began.

"Yogi found you! Oh gods, is he okay? I didn't even think about him yet. I'm completely ashamed of myself," she said, new tears forming in her eyes.

"Hey now, easy. You went through a lot, and you are still in shock. Give yourself a break," he said, wrapping her in his arms.

"But is he okay? Yogi was hurt, bleeding everywhere. He bit Stefan's hand right off, but Stefan clawed him—"

"Shhh. Yes, the big bear made it all the way to the Pride house, and he found me. I didn't realize he was hurt at first, but we got Mikey, the Pride healer, on it right away. He just called, and Yogi is going to make it. He'll have some new scars, but chicks dig scars, right?" he said, lightening the mood as she wiped her tears away and chuckled.

"Yo Pierce, got a second?" Hunter called, and she told him to go.

She needed a minute anyway.

"There you are, child."

"Uncle Uzzi!" she gasped, covering her heart with her hand.

"Sorry to startle you, dear," he replied.

His blue eyes were sparkling, and his white beard and hair looked bright in the still dark skies. Toni exhaled a breath, willing herself to calm down. He looked at her patiently and kindly, and she warmed inside. He really was a wonder, this magical match-making Witch.

"No, no, I am fine," she said.

"Good. Now, I know your siblings and mother and stepfather all saw you already, but they wanted to give you some space. Especially Adrianna. She feels particularly guilty, but I told your family I would see you and report back to them. So, are you okay?" Uncle Uzzi asked, concern marring his face.

"Well, Uncle Uzzi, really, I shouldn't be okay. I mean, I was setup at work, kidnapped, and almost forced to become some baby making factory for a madman who wanted to sell our cubs to a bunch of Shifter-hunting bastards. That's a lot for anyone," she said with a sigh.

"It certainly is. I am so sorry about the timing of all this. Here, I thought I had found the perfect mate for you and for Pierce. But if you need time, Antonetta, let me know and I will help break the news to him. He has already said he would wait—"

"Oh no! I mean, Uncle Uzzi, what happened tonight was crazy and scary and I hate that it happened. But I'm fine. Everyone I care about is okay. If there is one thing I am sure of, it's Pierce McDowd. He absolutely is my fated mate, and meeting him when I did was just as it was meant to be. I love him, Uncle Uzzi. Thank you so much for bringing us together," she said, and kissed the older man on the cheek.

"Ah! Hear that, *liebling?*" he asked aloud to the ghost of his dearly departed wife. "I guess timing really is everything."

Uncle Uzzi said his goodbyes and left for his next assignment, she imagined. Toni and Pierce were allowed to leave, with assurances he would not be charged with any crimes. Maggie Pierce had even called, concerned for Toni's well-being.

"Toni, I understand you might need a few days, but know we want you back at EWLP as soon as you can. Your job with us is always secure. I have personally comprised a team of auditors going through all our employee records to ensure a slip up like Bixby or Perry or whatever his name is, never happens again!"

"Thank you, Ms. Pierce, but my campaign will still need to be investigated if the things Bixby said were true—"

"Oh, they weren't. he got someone to pose as the real photographer, claiming those images were not his to use, but that was all fake. Just another charge pending against that bastard! The campaign is back up and running, and it is a smashing success. So, when can we expect you back?"

"Thank you so much for sharing that information with me," Toni replied, swallowing her relief. "But you know what? I think I will be using some of those vacation days I had saved and take some time off to be with my mate," she told the older woman, now CEO of Eat Well Live Proud.

Toni said her goodbyes after Ms. Pierce reassured her that she would let HR know. She stood leaning against a black walnut tree, just staring at her mate, who was talking to his Neta. As if he sensed her eyes on him, the big sexy Tiger turned his head.

His gaze found hers with that crooked smile she loved spread across his face. He ambled over, cupping her cheeks and nuzzling her nose in that show of affection all Big Cats loved.

"You ready to go, love?"

"Yes. Take me home, Pierce. I'm ready. I want you to claim me tonight."

Toni really was ready. It was time to claim her life and her future.

Prrrr.

Epilogue

Pierce was silent the entire drive to the house he'd recently built just down the road from the Pride House. He was so damn nervous he practically vibrated right out of the driver's side of the car he'd borrowed from Hunter.

His Neta had left him the keys, told him where he'd parked, and waved him away. A couple of agents from the DPCA gave them a lift in their ATVs to the vehicle when they'd finished answering questions, and Pierce was free to take Toni home.

He was a fucking jumble of mixed emotions, the least of which was not pure gratitude. Toni was safe, whole, and he had her back.

Thank the gods, the Fates, the universe, and Yogi.

Toni's stalker bear was going to be spoiled like no other ursine on the planet. He was already planning a huge rehabilitation pen in his backyard so the creature could live out his old age in peace.

After Mikey finished patching him up, he discovered the bear would have limited mobility in his front quarters from the injuries Stefan had given him. If left in the wild, he would likely not last the winter. The hell with that. Pierce had already asked Hunter about it, and the Neta agreed to sell him the lot next to his house.

Pierce was going to fence the entire thing off and build a huge rehab pen for Yogi, and who knew, maybe rescuing wildlife would become a thing with them. He'd already told his idea to Toni, and her reciprocal smile had dazzled him. But that was the last thing he'd said, and now the minutes were ticking away with too much silence between them.

Uncertainty filled him as he rolled to a stop in front of his house. The new cobblestone driveway he'd put in made faint bumping sounds beneath the tires, and the familiarity of that beat settled him a little.

Just a little.

"Wow, this is nice," Toni whispered, her golden

eyes wide as she leaned forward and looked out his side of the window.

She smelled like forest and fur, blood and hurt, but beneath all that she was peaches and honey. She was Toni, his Toni. Unable to resist, Pierce reached out and gathered her in his arms, and she shuddered, clinging tight to him.

"I thought I lost you," he whispered his greatest fear aloud, closing his eyes tight.

"You didn't. I'm here. I am right here with you. Take me inside, show me your home."

Pierce nodded, using the distraction of giving her the grand tour of *McDowd Mansion*, as he jokingly referred to his home, to get out of his own head. He helped her out of the car, and she held onto his hand as they walked down the pathway to the front door.

"This is nice. Big, roomy, and it smells new," she remarked, and he winked.

"Finished construction a few months ago, I guess my Tiger was more bent on finding a mate than I knew," he confessed.

Toni smiled, leaning on him as he pressed the code into the specialized lock. Pierce stopped her from going in. head cocked, he had the sudden urge to do something old-fashioned, and silly, maybe. But he wanted to do it, nonetheless.

"What is it?" she asked.

"Come here," he whispered and lifted her up, princess style.

Toni melted into him, her eyes going all soft and sweet. She reached up, kissing his lips as he stepped over the threshold with her in his arms. Gods, he loved her like this, submissive and supple. But he also loved her when she was fierce and furious. There were a million different shades of Toni Golden, and Pierce didn't know all of them yet, but he was looking damn forward to learning each one.

"I love you," he growled.

"I love you, too."

He took her on the tour of the first floor. There was a large living room, kitchen, laundry, a full bathroom, and a dining room. The second floor was made up of the bedrooms. There were three smaller units with two more bathrooms between them. He saved the main bedroom, which would be theirs, he hoped, for last.

"Pierce?"

"Yeah?"

"Do you suppose I could take a shower?"

"Of course," he told her, leading the way to the private bathroom connected to the main bedroom.

"This is huge," she said, smiling as she took in the

sunken bathtub on one end of the room, and the enormous shower with its three heads and tiled walls.

There was no door to the shower, but both the shower floor and the rest of the bathroom floor had drains in place just in case water escaped. The colors were all earth tones to go with the natural stone tile. The tile was anti-slip, natural stone, to avoid accidents.

Pierce watched Toni spin in a slow circle, a hint of a smile on her face. His heart pounded. It shouldn't matter, since things could always be changed, but he really wanted her to like his house.

"This place is beautiful, Pierce," she said, meeting his gaze at last.

"Thank you," he replied. "Here lemme turn on the water," he mumbled, and showed her the faucets before turning the water on warm.

Toni blushed a pretty pink color. She mumbled her thanks and started untying the blanket at her waist.

"Oh, I'm sorry. You probably want privacy," he said, and moved to leave.

"No! I mean, no, I don't want privacy. I want you," she told him shyly and Pierce almost fell to his knees.

"I don't want to rush you," he whispered, afraid to break the fragile moment.

"Please, I need you," she said, her eyes blazing gold.

And like the first time, she stripped her clothes off slowly, holding his gaze while she backed into the stream of water cascading down from the shower. Pierce's growl shook the whole room. He stripped quickly, following her into the shower.

"You make the moves here, Toni," he told her. "You are in control."

She smiled then, with no reservations at all. So beautiful and bright, it lit up the whole damn night. She took some shampoo, ran it through her hair, then turned so he could finish the job. Pierce took to it immediately.

Condition, rinse, repeat. Same with her body. Toni sighed under his ministrations, moaning when his touches went from mechanical to methodical. That's when she started to purr and Pierce about lost his damned mind.

"Pierce."

Toni moaned his name as his teeth grazed the skin over her throat. He turned her to him, lifting her in his arms, grateful for the fact he'd washed himself off hurriedly when he was bathing her.

Lifting her in his arms, he grabbed a fluffy peach towel and draped it over them, barely making it to the bed. Lips smashed together, they crashed onto the mattress, Pierce making sure he didn't crush her.

"I like the weight of you on top of me," she whispered, spreading her thighs to accommodate his bigger frame.

"Toni, Toni," he repeated her name like a litany, over and over again as her heat encompassed him.

There was no hurry. No rush. This joining as precious and potent as their first. Golden eyes glittered in the darkness of the room, her Lioness joining the fray as he moved within her, touching every inch of her he could reach. From his hands clasping hers over her head to his chest smashed up against hers. Toni wrapped her legs around his waist, rolling her hips to meet his rocking, shallow thrusts.

He'd never felt anything like this, and he couldn't get enough. She reached up, nipping his lip with her teeth as their moves grew more urgent. This was more than sex, more than mating, this was a conversion of beings. A joining and reshaping of two people made for each other, for each other.

Was it too short a time for that? Maybe. But what did Pierce care what anyone else thought?

This moment was everything. Toni gasped aloud, and he followed the sound, moving in tune with her needy whispers and throaty grunts.

"That's good, pretty girl. Tell me what you like, what you need," he praised her.

"Want you to mark me, Pierce. Claim me. Make me yours," she told him, eyes on his, her nails digging into his hips.

Fuck. Yes.

He'd been holding back, not sure if the trauma of the night had influenced her earlier. Pierce was all set to delay. But not now. Not when she was looking at him with her Lioness in her eyes and begging him to claim her.

"Mine," he snarled.

The slapping sounds of their sex grew louder, and Pierce's muscles strained and flexed with every swivel, pump, and thrust. All his efforts were worth it, though. He struck, marking her the second she came, shouting his name. Toni's scream became muffled, and Pierce felt pain and burning on his left pectoral. That was quickly followed by bliss so earth shattering, he almost passed out.

"Now, you're mine, too."

He felt her smile more than saw it, since his eyes were still closed. Pierce's movements slowed, but aftershocks of their orgasm went on and on a few minutes more. His whole body throbbed and pulsed, and he knew nothing could ever feel as good as claiming Toni.

"Pierce?" Toni whispered, her warm breath tickling his sensitive skin.

"Yeah?"

"I'm glad I waited for you."

Love. Love. LOVE.

He felt it in their matebond. Heard it in her voice. Toni really loved Pierce, and he loved her right back.

"Me too, pretty girl. I don't think our timing could have been more purrfect."

Early the next morning. Toni poured a second cup of coffee, still full from the amazing Belgian waffle breakfast Pierce had made her, when the doorbell rang.

"Who's that?" she asked her mate, who was bending over the dishwasher, giving her a lovely view of his assets.

Yummy man.

"Huh? I don't know. You stay. I'll go check."

She nodded and sighed, drinking a good sip. Of

course, that was when Pierce returned carrying an enormous basket filled to bursting with a ridiculous amount of X-rated paraphernalia. Toni snorted coffee out of her nose, she was laughing so hard.

"Dear new bro-in-law, here's some from your new family to keep Toni the Tiger lover happy. Hope you're into nipple clips—Toni, what the heck? Are you okay?"

He chuckled, dropping the basket on the table, and grabbing her some paper towels. Toni gasped, trying to catch her breath.

"I'm gonna kill my sisters," she said.

"Don't bother. We'll get 'em back. Besides, I think I saw some peach flavored edible oils. You know I love peaches," he growled playfully.

"Mmm, that sounds promising," she replied, and giggled when he picked her up and tossed her over his shoulder.

Life with Pierce was never going to be boring, and even better, the male was supremely confident in her ability to make her own decisions, handle herself, and let him know when she needed or wanted something from him. They'd already promised to never stop communicating with one another, and far as she was concerned, that gave them a leg up in this whole fated mates thing.

"Pierce, what about family? Are you going to be okay if I want to wait?" she asked after they were all sweaty and sated and completely high on one another.

"Whatever decision you make, I will be fine with it. Whether you want to remain on heat suppressants, or try for cubs, or adopt, or not have kids and just adopt a million cats to keep Yogi company, I am completely on board."

"You say that but—"

"But nothing, Toni, *you* are my family. I love you."

"I love you, too. I promise to talk to you before anything. This is our family, Pierce, we both make the decisions."

Then he smiled at her, and Toni knew she got it right this time.

***

Elsewhere...

. . .

Uncle Uzzi shook his head and sighed.

Some Shifters just could not accept their fate. Take Carter, the cowardly Lion, ex-limo driver.

"You thinking about that Cat again," Richard asked, prepping a nice pot of chamomile tea for Uzzi.

"I just don't know why he is fighting it so hard," Uzzi replied, reaching out to snag one of Richard's delicious lemon shortbread cookies.

"I see you sneaking a cookie, Uzzi, now shame on you. What would Betty say?"

"My libeling appreciated my sweet tooth," he countered, nibbling the delectable treat.

"Yes, well, she also would have told you to let the young Lion Shifter go about his business. He'll come around when the time is right."

The old Witch sighed and flicked the corner of one of the new business cards he'd had made up. *Uncle Uzzi's Magical Matchmaking Service* was scrawled across the thick white card stock in bold blue letters.

He supposed Richard was right. Besides, there was always another client waiting for his insights.

But Carter would do wise to beware, the Fates

were liable to take away that which they had bestowed if ignored for too long.

"Beware indeed, little pussy," he mumbled.

"What was that?" Richard asked over the whistling kettle.

"Nothing, Richard. Not yet anyway. Now, let's have some tea!"

T *he end.*

Did you enjoy this story?

Look for the rest of the Maverick Pride Tales on my website here: https://www.cdgorri.com/series/maverick-pride-tales/.
Or check out the Dire Wolf Mates here: https://www.cdgorri.com/series/dire-wolf-mates.
Happy reading!

Beware... Here Be Dragons!

The Falk Clan Tales began as my stories surrounding four dragon Brothers and how they find their one true mates, but when a long lost brother arrives on the scene, followed by a few more Shifters...what can I say? The more the merrier!

Each Dragon's chest is marked with his rose, the magical link to his heart and his magic. They each have a matching gemstone to go with it.

She's given up on love. But he's just begun.

In The Dragon's Valentine we meet the eldest Falk brother, Callius. He is on a mission to find a Castle and his one true mate, one he can trust with his diamond rose....

His heart is frozen. Can she change his mind about love?

In The Dragon's Christmas Gift our attention shifts to Alexsander, the youngest brother of the four. He has resigned himself to a life alone, until he meets *her*.

Some wounds run deep. Can a Dragon's heart be unbroken?

The Dragon's Heart is the story of Edric Falk who has vowed never to love again, but that changes when he meets his feisty mate, Joselyn Curacao.

She just wants a little fun. He's looking for a lifetime.

We finally meet Nikolai Falk and his sexy Shifter mate in The Dragon's Secret.

She doesn't believe in fairytales, until a Dragon comes knocking on her door.

Meet Castor Falk, the long lost brother of our original four Dragons, and his sassy mate Josette. The Dragon's Treasure is full of adventure and laughs.

Nothing can surprise this six hundred-year-old Dragon, except maybe her.

Devine Graystone meets his match in Sunny Daye, an irrepressible Wolf Shifter with a heart of gold. Read their story in The Dragon's Surprise.

He's a hardcore realist until she dares him to dream.

Nicholas Gravestone doesn't know what to think when he spies Minerva Lykos on the property his Dragon covets. Can this unlikely pair come to a truce? Find out in The Dragon's Dream.

Thanks for reading.

xoxo,

C.D.

*Dragon Mates & Dragon Mates 2 boxed sets are now available in hardcover, paperback, and ebook. *Get a discount when you buy direct!*

Have you met the Barvale Clan Bears?

Looking for a Paranormal Romance series that is loads of growly fun?

Meet the Barvale Clan first in the Bear Claw Tales! A complete shifter romance series about 4 brothers who discover and need to win their fated mates!
Titles are:
Bearly Breathing
Bearly There
Bearly Tamed
Bearly Mated

Followed by two more spin off series, the Barvale Clan Tales, featuring:
Polar Opposites

Polar Outbreak
Polar Compound
Polar Curve

and, of course, the Barvale Holiday Tales, beginning
with A Bear For Christmas
Hers to Bear
Thank You Beary Much
&
Bearing Gifts!
Look for more of these sexy, heartwarming holiday
inspired tales soon!

No cliffhangers. Steamy PNR fun.
Get a discount when you buy direct!
Go and read your next happily ever after today!

Other Titles by C.D. Gorri

Paranormal Romance Books:

Macconwood Pack Novel Series:

Charley's Christmas Wolf: A Macconwood Pack Novel 1

Cat's Howl: A Macconwood Pack Novel 2

Code Wolf: A Macconwood Pack Novel 3

The Witch and The Werewolf: A Macconwood Pack Novel 4

To Claim a Wolf: A Macconwood Pack Novel 5

Conall's Mate: A Macconwood Pack Novel 6

Her Solstice Wolf: A Macconwood Pack Novel 7

Werewolf Fever: A Macconwood Pack Novel 8

Also available in 2 ebook boxed sets:

The Macconwood Pack Volume 1

The Macconwood Pack Volume 2

Polar Compound: A Barvale Clan Tale 3

Polar Curve: A Barvale Clan Tale 4

Also available in a boxed set:

The Barvale Clan Tales (Books 1-4)

Barvale Holiday Tales:

A Bear For Christmas

Hers To Bear

Thank You Beary Much

Bearing Gifts

Bearly Friends

Also available in a boxed set:

The Barvale Holiday Tales (Books 1-3)

Purely Paranormal Romance Books:

Marked by the Devil: Purely Paranormal Romance Books

Mated to the Dragon King: Purely Paranormal Romance Books

Claimed by the Demon: Purely Paranormal Romance Books

Christmas with a Devil, a Dragon King, & a Demon: Purely Paranormal Romance Books

Vampire Lover: Purely Paranormal Romance Books

Grizzly Lover: Purely Paranormal Romance Books

Christmas With Her Chupacabra: Purely Paranormal Romance Books

Purely Paranormal Romance Books Anthology Volume 1

The Wardens of Terra:

Bound by Air: The Wardens of Terra Book 1

Star Kissed: A Wardens of Terra Short

Waterlocked: The Wardens of Terra Book 2

Moon Kissed: A Wardens of Terra Short

*Now in a boxed set and in audio!

The Maverick Pride Tales:

Purrfectly Mated

Purrfectly Kissed

Purrfectly Trapped

Purrfectly Caught

Purrfectly Naughty

Purrfectly Bound

Purrfectly Paired

Purrfectly Timed

Dire Wolf Mates:

Shake That Sass

Breaking Sass

Pinch of Sass

Kickin' Sass

Wyvern Protection Unit:

Gift Wrapped Protector: WPU 1

Tempted By Her Protector: WPU 2

Alien Protector: WPU 3

Unexpected Protector: WPU4

Jersey Sure Shifters/EveL Worlds:

Chinchilla and the Devil: A FUCN'A Book

Sammi and the Jersey Bull: A FUCN'A Book

Mouse and the Ball: A FUCN'A Book

Chicken and the Paparazzi: A FUCN'A Book

Jersey Sure Shifters Books 1-3 anthology

The Guardians of Chaos:

Wolf Shield: Guardians of Chaos Book1

Dragon Shield: Guardians of Chaos Book 2

Stallion Shield: Guardians of Chaos Book 3

Panther Shield: Guardians of Chaos 4

Witch Shield: Guardians of Chaos 5

Vampire Shield: Guardians of Chaos 6

Guardians of Chaos Volume 1 Books 1-3

Guardians of Chaos Volume 2 Books 4-6

Twice Mated Tales

Doubly Claimed

Doubly Bound

Doubly Tied

Twice Mated Tales Anthology

Hearts of Stone Series

Shifter Mountain: Hearts of Stone 1

Shifter City: Hearts of Stone 2

Shifter Village: Hearts of Stone 3

Hearts of Stone Books 1-3 Anthology

Accidentally Undead Series

Fangs For Nothin'

Moongate Island Tales

Moongate Island Mate

Moongate Island Christmas Claim

Mated in Hope Falls

Mated by Moonlight

Sweet As Candy

###

###

Hunter Moon: A Grazi Kelly Novel Book 2

Rebel Moon: A Grazi Kelly Novel Book 3

Winter Moon: A Grazi Kelly Novel Book 4

Chasing The Moon: A Grazi Kelly Short 5

Blood Moon: A Grazi Kelly Novel 6

*Get all 6 books NOW AVAILABLE IN A BOXED SET:

The Complete Grazi Kelly Novel Series

The Angela Tanner Files

Casting Magic: The Angela Tanner Files 1

Keeping Magic: The Angela Tanner Files 2

*The Angela Tanner Files Paperback 2 Book omnibus

G'Witches Magical Mysteries Series

Co-written with P. Mattern

G'Witches

G'Witches 2: The Harpy Harbinger

G'Witches 3: Summoning Secrets

Witches of Westwood Academy

Co-written with Gina Kincade

Water Witch

Air Witch

Fire Witch

Earth Witch

Excerpt from Sealed Fate

It was snowing, but that wasn't new. Konstantin huddled beneath the broken concrete and waited for the big men to leave. He'd heard the shouting from all the way down the street when he'd gone to pick up his little sister, Alina, from her ballet lessons.

Though his family was poor, Papa and Mama sacrificed much so she could learn to dance. Konstantin was proud of his sister's already budding talent at just six years old. She'd been a surprise to the older couple whose son was already a teenager, but they all doted on her.

Konstantin was almost old enough to work the docks with his father, but Mama insisted he finish school. At nearly seven feet tall and still growing, it was proving difficult to remain unnoticed by the local bratva. That was something his mother feared more than anything.

"Be a good boy, Konstantin. Stay away from the gangs, and criminals," she'd told often him.

After all, it was his dealings with the local crime bosses that had left his Papa with a permanent limp and physical disabilities from the multiple toes and fingers that were missing from his feet and hands. Shifters could recover from many wounds and injuries, but not amputations. That was something even their enhanced healing abilities could not overcome.

The screams got louder, and Konstantin picked up Alina who'd just started to cry. The sounds were coming from the building where his family rented an apartment from Ivanovich. The head of the local bratva had many slums on the city where he took advantage of the many poor Shifter families.

His inner beast scratched and roared, but he was no match for the many members of the bratva waiting for their boss outside. Instead of facing them and risking Alina's life, he covered her mouth with his hands and hid them both in the cellar of the neighboring building.

The old man was yelling about missing rents and

late payments. He was going to use Konstantin's father as an example, or worse, take it out on his mother. That was something, he could not allow.

"Alina, will you stay here? Hidden for me, yes?" he asked his baby sister.

Blue eyes clear as the sky looked up at him, swimming with tears. She nodded her head, already older than her six years and he nodded, cursing roughly under his breath. He prayed he was not too late.

By the time he reached the apartment the men were gone, and his mother was wailing over the prone body of his father. Papa was gone. Killed by the bastards who ruled over all of them.

"Konstantin!" she cried, standing up and going to him, still covered in her mate's blood. "You must run. Go to your Uncle. Je will put you on a ship---"

"What about you? Alina?"

"Where is she?"

"In the basement next door. Let me get her," he said, frantic with worry.

"Yes, get her. I will pack."

When he once again returned to the apartment, he found the neighbors gathered. They shook their heads and turned their backs on him and his family, shunning them even as his father's body grew cold on their kitchen floor. Anger surged, but his mother was there, stopping it before he could blow like a steam engine.

"Come. Now. There is no time," she said, handing him a suitcase and taking the whimpering child from his arms.

They ran through the street, ducking in alleys, and moving faster then the humans around them. Tiger Shifters had night vision and traversing through the ice slicked alleys was quick work for them. They reached his Uncle's house in no time at all.

"You've come," Uncle Petyr said, grabbing his sister in a quick hug.

The man took his niece and handed her off to his wife who cuddled the child close. All the adults were trying not to cry, but Konstantin could feel their grief. Shared it with them.

"Can you get him out of here?" Mama begged.

"Only the boy. I am sorry," Uncle Petyr said.

"It is good. he will make a good life and we will come later," she said, nodding. "Okay Konstantin? Yes?"

"I want to stay with you," he said, a boy's dream.

"No, I won't let them have you too," Mama cred, holding him tight to her breast. "I love you son, but I need you to live. Here, there is only death waiting for you. Now go. Be strong. Be the man I know you can be. We will be together one day."

"We go now," Uncle Petyr said, grabbing the suitcase and taking Konstantin's hand.

"Mama? Mama!"

"Come now, boy. Be quiet or you will bring those monsters here."

That fact shut him up faster than if his Uncle had slapped him. Konstantin looked one last time at his mother and sister, who'd returned to her side. He waved and nodded, biting back his own tears, then he left his Uncle's apartment. And Russia.

And he never looked back.

Grab the rest of the story here: https://www. cdgorri.com/books/sealed-fate

Excerpt from *Unexpected Protector*

"Are you fucking kidding me?"

Jennifer Dylluan scrubbed her face with her hands, and yes, she might've screamed aloud while doing so. The sound was more screech than scream, come to think of it, probably because of the enormous, ornery, and extremely orotund owl resting inside the otherwise completely agreeable female.

"What the fuck, Medjed!" she snapped, but he had no reply.

The female had called for him moments ago, but even as he stood there waiting for her to look at him once more, she seemed displeased. Her voice still echoed through the halls.

It was, of course, his name. As the most recent

member of the Wyvern Protection Unit, the only non-Wyvern to join, in fact, Medjed had wondered when he would be called to duty.

"I swear to Christ, man, you are the bane of my existence," she muttered, shaking her head. "And really, that is saying something, considering I'm the liaison between the DPCA and the four worst mannered Shifters on the entire fucking planet!"

The DPCA he knew was the acronym for the Department of Paranormal Creatures and Activity, and those four Shifters who she claimed were always giving her a headache, were his new blood brothers. Jasper, Larimar, Heliodore, and Zircon Wessex of the Wyvern Protection Unit.

But nothing could make him understand why their liaison, Ms. Jennifer Dylluan was calling for him one minute then proclaiming him top on her *menace to society* list, which was apparently a thing one did not wish to be on.

"I, Warrior of the House of Osiris, Sword of the Underworld, Deliverer for the God of the Dead, Punisher of the Unworthy, Demigod, and Hero, worshipped by hundreds of thousands in the Ancient World—me, I, *Medjed*, am here as you have bid me, Jennifer Dylluan." He finished with a low bow before returning to his full height, which was an impressive six and a half feet.

Debates over whether he was a Demon, or a minor God, had run rampant in the secret government office where they worked, so Medjed often took it upon himself to use as many of his titles as he could remember. But Jennifer did not seem capable of caring less. He frowned, furrowing his eyebrows as the female heaved a great sigh.

"I cannot go on like this. Not when other assignments are demanding my attention," she murmured, eyes cast at the ceiling.

Medjed frowned thoughtfully. Jennifer was so stressed. Her animal, too. That was not good for a female. Especially not one who was a vital part of his new work and family of his heart.

It was clear what the problem was. Jennifer Dylluan needed a mate. Medjed was willing to ease any physical aches she might have, but he wondered if perhaps one of his new Wyvern blood brothers would not be better suited. In fact, there was one particular brother who was likely the reason the poor female was having fits.

"*Ohmyfuckinggawd!* He is still standing there like that," she mumbled to herself, shaking with emotion.

Medjed frowned. The female was worrying him.

The Great-horned Owl inside of her growled unhappily as her gaze flitted back to the pile of paperwork on her desk.

"My fault, right? I mean, I called in the naked ass mofo, and you know what they say, speak of the devil and he will appear," she growled some more, taking a bottle out of her bottom drawer.

Medjed sneezed when she started spraying the floral perfume. It was simply too much for his sensitive olfactory senses.

"Naked as a jaybird. Smelling like a damned cinnamon bun. Leaving a trail of fucking sand everywhere," she muttered, moving to the closet to retrieve a broom.

He wisely remained mute. Yes, Medjed had arrived in his usual golden splendor via sand cloud that gave way to his impressive form. It was how he always traveled.

He waited while Jennifer swept, sprayed, and cursed him out to her heart's content. He would never engage a female in battle, lest she try to maim him, at which point he would evade attack. Never would he raise a hand with harmful intent to the fairer sex.

"And this, really, this is how you sign things," she

snapped, bringing his attention to his signature on some forms she had sent him.

"It is my signature, Jennifer Dylluan."

"It is a dildo, Medjed. A fucking dildo!"

"It is not this thing. It is my hieroglyph," he growled, trying to hold his temper.

Yes, his hieroglyph had caused some amusement amongst his new people. And after he'd been shown modern mechanical phalluses, he had to agree. It was shaped rather like a, well, like a dildo with eyes and feet.

It was the shape of the thing, long and conical in form, that apparently caused so much merriment. The fact he did carry a rather spectacular package was not lost on him. He was rather splendidly formed.

Not that Jennifer had ever mentioned interest, though he would admit she had looked twice. Totally understandable. Medjed was not ashamed of his body.

"For the love of fuck, put on some damned clothes!" she snapped, trying her best not to stare at the currently flaccid and yet still enormous phallus that hung between his thighs.

"And that thing is why your hieroglyph resembles a fucking dildo," she muttered rudely.

"Sorry, great *amoula*. I had no time to dress. I was in the divine washing basin you call a *bathtub*," he explained.

She narrowed her eyes, and he waved his hand, clothing himself in a very short, royal blue, velour robe.

"I told you a million times, Medjed. We wear clothes here. When I call you, dress first, then sandman your way in," she grumbled and shuffled through paperwork.

"I will do as you say, *amoula*. Now, why have you called on me? What can I help with today?"

He smiled, calling her the Egyptian word for owl as a sign of respect for both her creature and her wisdom. She had told him once she thought it sounded pretty, so he deemed it appropriate to continue using the pet name.

Jennifer groaned aloud and banged her head on the desk. The *amoula* was distressed.

"What am I going to do with you, you maniac? Help? He wants to help! You want to help?"

"Of course," he said, staring at her warily.

"Of course? Did you say *of course*?"

"Um, Jennifer—"

"Help. You want to help. Is that what you were doing when you conjured a sandstorm to swallow a local fast food dive when the owner refused to cook the deer you brought him? Hmm? Were you helping then?" she shouted.

"He was being obtuse, and it was a fresh kill. I did not desire to imbibe the frozen fat filled mystery meat he called a *pa-tty*," he explained as if this was perfectly reasonable.

"I see and were you helping when you kidnapped a woman on her wedding day and took her to a hotel in Atlantic City where you then engaged in sexual activities for three days before either of you came up for air?" she continued, her voice growing higher in both pitch and volume.

"The woman did not wish to be married. She confessed it to me the night before at her *bach-elore-ette* party. I merely did as she asked and showed her true physical pleasure before she tied herself to the short and stout dentist, she was binding herself to for eternity. Three days was her decision, I could've stayed in bed for weeks living on nothing but the taste of her pleasure," he grinned wickedly, and Jennifer did not bother to stifle her groan.

"What is it? Did I do something wrong?"

"Medjed, you are completely maddening. Wait, did you say you could live on a woman's pleasure for weeks?"

"Weeks," he repeated, noting the curious glint in her eyes.

Truthfully, if she were free, if her heart had not belonged to another as he suspected it did, perhaps he might show her it was no challenge at all. Alas, Jennifer Dylluan was not his.

A week of purely carnal, sexual bliss always sounded great to Medjed. but his heart would not be in it. Truth was, he'd been feeling rather restless lately.

Ever since Jasper's mate, Carolina, had freed him from the tablet where he had been confined, Medjed felt the emptiness inside of him growing. The beast that was loneliness refused to let him be.

He did not even want to entertain the notion of what he feared he must do. But it was weighing on him, heavy at that.

Jennifer was lucky. Her heart was already taken, even if the man in question was unaware. But for Medjed, he had no notion where to find his fated one.

Do not go there, he told himself.

It was too dark and dangerous a tunnel to travel. Especially now when he had a duty to attend.

"So, have we cleared everything up, *amoula*? I wish to go back to my tub and to finish watching the moving pictures Kimberley Wessex has shown me on the *Hall-march* channel. She called them *holly-day moo-vees*, I believe."

"You are watching the Holiday Movie Marathon on the Hallmark Channel?" she asked, gaping at him.

"Yes. I find it fascinating. Except, well, this *San Ta Claws* devil seems like the worst kind of villain, Jennifer. Surely, he is being investigated by your offices," Medjed stated, moving where he could make his exit free and clear of furniture. Traveling by sand did cause a bit of a mess, he admitted sheepishly.

"No," she yelled, stopping him in his tracks, "I have a new assignment for you."

"Yes," he said expectantly.

"But first, why do you think Santa is a devil?" she asked, clearly allowing her curiosity to get the better of her.

"It is obvious," Medjed stated, unbelieving she would even need to ask. "*San Ta Claws* is a burglar and a madman. Who else would spy on innocents and threaten them with naughty lists and coal? So, is that my assignment?" he asked with glee.

"Is what your assignment?"

"Am I to track down and destroy that monster of monsters, the *San Ta Claws* himself?" he asked.

"No! God no," she said. "But speaking of the North Pole, do you own a coat?" Jennifer smirked.

G rab the rest of the story here: https://www.cdgorri.com/books/unexpected-protector

Excerpt from Purrfectly Mated

How the fuck did I wind up here?

It was all Elissa could do not to slam her face down on the table as she pondered that question for the umpteenth time since leaving her cozy Hoboken apartment to go on this so called date.

"So, babe," the over-stuffed, heavily-cologned, and downright fugly man said.

Her date of the evening looked like something out of a bad sitcom as he tried to lean over the stained tablecloth of the rundown hotel buffet room, he'd driven two hours to get to. Waggling his caterpillar-like eyebrows, he gave her the once over and Elissa's skin crawled.

Oh, hell no.

"I got a room upstairs, you know, for *after*," he told her, nodding his head, and biting his lower lip in a manner she assumed he thought was provocative.

At best, it was nauseating.

FML.

How was this guy Elissa's date for the evening? What had she done to deserve this?

Little Gianni. Yup, that was how he'd introduced himself. And here she was. On a blind date with a guy who had the word 'little' in front of his name.

Well, what did she expect? Roses and champagne? In this economy? She didn't know where Cinder-fucking-ella got her prince, but it sure as fuck wasn't in Jersey.

Elissa could only blame herself for agreeing to go on this blind date. Initially, the whole Little Gianni fiasco had been intended for her roommate.

Wait a second. Scratch that thought.

It *was* all Gretchen's fault. That ungrateful cow!

She tried to play it off like she was some sweet little homegrown maiden. Oh, just wait till Elissa got home. Gretchen was never going to hear the end of it.

She owed Elissa. Big time. Like a whole month of

washing the dishes big time. The rat trap they shared in her hometown of Hoboken was all the two women could afford, and for the most part, they got along just fine.

In fact, they'd grown to be close friends over the three years they'd lived together. It was the only reason she'd ever agreed to this date from Hell.

Elissa sighed and looked over at Little Gianni. Maybe he wasn't all that bad?

"*BEEEELLLLLLLLCHHH!* 'Scuse me, doll. Better out, am I right?"

Gianni winked and Elissa wished for a black hole to open up and swallow her up right through the floor.

OMFG.

The man just burped out loud like he was in a frat boy belting contest, only those days passed him up about thirty years ago.

For fuck's sake. Gretchen, you so owe me.

Elissa cursed her roommate and tried not to groan. But Little Gianni wasn't quite done. The grown ass man lifted his leg and let one rip.

Right. Fucking. There.

Elissa was going to die before the end of the night.

Literally.

This is what you get when you do a friend a favor without asking for details! Idiota!

The voice of her Italian grandmother sounded in her brain. She tried to ignore it, willing herself not to wince at the man while he sucked air, and who knows what else, noisily through his coffee-stained teeth.

Ew. So gross.

That was the perfect word to describe it. The only word, in fact. The entire date was just so fucking gross. She still couldn't believe her sweet little roommate from Iowa, *Gretchen Kaepernick*, she of the wispy hair and baby blues, had set her up with this guy!

What the actual fuck was up with that?

Little Gianni was a slob. Actually, he looked just like her Uncle Nico, and that was not a good thing. Seriously, not good at all.

He wore his hair slicked back in a too tight ponytail that emphasized his rapidly receding hairline. As if that wasn't enough to put her off, he was sporting an enormous paunch. Now, being a curvy girl, Elissa appreciated food and was in no way against men showing the same appreciation.

She liked bigger men. Always had. But bigger did not mean you had to be sloppy. Little Gianni's stomach was literally hanging out from under a tight tan golf shirt that had definitely seen better days.

The man didn't even look like he had ever played a sport of any kind. With it, he wore brown poly-ester pants that were three inches above his ankles and unbuttoned at the waist.

He didn't look like he tried at all for this date. What kind of guy did that? His shirt collar was bent and wrinkled, and all three buttons were open to his chest, revealing a mat of oily, dark hair and pimples.

Somehow, he'd managed to tuck the back of the shirt in, but the front simply would not hold in that stomach. What worried her more were the tight brown pants.

As he sat back and stretched, she wondered if she should take cover. They looked like they were one bite from exploding off his body. Elissa shuddered at the image.

Please God, if You have an ounce of mercy, don't let that happen, she prayed.

"Hang on, doll, I gotta take this," he said, and turned to answer his cell phone.

It was ringing to the tune of '70s disco music she

hadn't heard since the last family reunion. Her eyes kept going to the huge stain on the front of his shirt. It was a little game she liked to call *what the hell is that*.

Coffee, she guessed.

"Up your ass, Bruno. I gotta have it by Monday," he cursed into the receiver.

Elissa winced at the spectacle he was making of them both. There were only a handful of people there, but still.

Deep breaths.

Ew. Maybe not.

She coughed as the strong body spray, that he'd obviously used a ton of in lieu of a shower, bad move in her opinion, invaded her lungs.

Oh, this was so bad.

Elissa was, by no means, a snob. But this guy looked like he'd stepped out of a bad 1980s mafia spoof film. What's worse, he kept smacking his lips together as he hung up the phone and looked her over from head to chest.

Thank fuck for the table, she thought, wishing she could hide her bosoms from his view.

"Sssss," he hissed, like it was sexy or something.

She just grimaced. Elissa might be able to forgive a lot of quirks, but she hated mouth noises. Really hated them. It was a super pet peeve of hers. Never mind his totally inappropriate and unwelcomed leer.

She started counting the minutes, willing the date to be over already. Plenty of people would tell her she shouldn't be so choosy, but really? She was not this desperate.

Not yet anyway.

So, she was curvy and a little mouthy too. But was it wrong to want a man with good table manners? Even if men were thin on the ground for someone like her.

As a chef, she'd worked in a lot of restaurants and even as a personal cook for professional couples. She'd seen her fair share of unhappy couples and downright uncomfortable marriages. But as far as she was concerned, all relationships went downhill when good table manners were dismissed.

Good manners were merely a sign that a person was thoughtful and respectful. At least, that was what Nonna had told her. Gianni here had clearly missed that lesson as a child. Elissa had to work not to groan in disgust as he slurped a raw clam down his gullet.

Shudder.

Was there no end to his feeding? That's what it reminded her of. Feeding time at the zoo.

OMG. That was rude, she scolded herself. But it wasn't like she said it out loud.

All she wanted to do was go home. At least she was comfortable. *She'd* worn her softest pair of black leggings for this disaster date, paired with one of her favorite tunics on top.

It was dark green with tiny black buttons down the front and showed just the right amount of cleavage. She'd gone for neat and tidy as opposed to downright sexy.

Good call, in her opinion. Elissa looked perfectly fine for a nice *getting to know you* dinner, which is what she thought she was getting when her roommate asked her to step in for her on a blind date that one of her best client's had set up for her.

Elissa shuddered now, thinking how good old Gianni here would've reacted to the red dress and heels she'd contemplated before checking the weather report.

Gulp.

The lewd man was already salivating, and she was so not having it. Fending off his unwanted advances was not how she wanted to finish the night.

Ew again.

Elissa shivered, slightly chilled despite the fact

they were indoors. It was a cold, gloomy evening, and the forecast called for even more rain later that night. Not at all unusual for this time of year in the Garden State.

November was always chilly in the evenings, rainy too. Elissa tended to run warm, but she was glad she'd brought a jacket with her. Especially since her date refused to turn the heat on in the car.

When she'd asked, he'd looked offended and told her it wasted gas.

Um. Okay.

She checked her phone. It was only seven o'clock, but the two hour drive was still ahead of them. Maybe they could make it home before ten if they left soon.

Ugh. Did he just blow his nose?

"Allergies, doll. Say, you gonna eat that?" he asked before scooping a fry from her dish and swallowing it down.

Elissa was gonna kill her roomie. Gretchen was a hair and nail stylist. A lot of her clients were elderly, and they just loved her. They were always offering to set her up on blind dates with their nephews and grandsons.

Mostly, the sweet old ladies were kind. They swore they could find her curvy roommate the right man, assuming she was single because she was new to town. Well, when Elissa got home tonight, she was going to tell Gretchen she needed to fire the old lady who set this date up from being her client.

Like *ASAP*.

No one who liked Gretchen would've sent her out with this guy. Gianni reached over and touched her hand and Elissa pulled back, reaching for the napkin.

Gross.

"I sure hope you ain't a cold one, doll," he said, shaking his head.

"What?"

"Ain't gonna matter. I know just what you need, doll."

She was still wiping the greasy residue he'd transferred to her skin from the food he ate sans utensils. This was too much. Elissa was beyond uncomfortable with all the leering and bad attempts at innuendo.

Plus, she was starving. One look at the dump he'd taken her to, and she knew she could never eat there. The chef in her wouldn't allow it.

To think they drove two hours for this! She'd practically frozen to death in his maroon Cadillac, listening to a CD of the Rat Pack, while Gianni crooned loudly, and off key, to the music.

Normally, she was a fan of the famous group of legendary singers. Having grown up in Hoboken, she couldn't not be a Sinatra fan. Though, to be honest, Dean Martin had always been her favorite.

Still, Elissa was a firm believer that there were just some people you did not try to imitate. Especially not if you were Little Gianni. While he was belting his heart out, he'd been trying to get his right hand on her thigh. She'd asked him politely to stop.

Twice.

Then she'd been forced to try something a little more drastic. Like spilling her hot tea on the offending hand the third time he'd tried it. Finally, he'd removed his hand from her leg. Not making a fourth attempt, which she was grateful for.

Elissa should've taken that behavior as a sign and gotten out of the car. But no. She'd wanted to do Gretchen a solid. So, against her better judgement, she gave the creep another chance.

Idiota, her grandmother's voice echoed in her brain again.

The old woman had loved her. Elissa knew that without a doubt. She'd raised her after her own parents had passed on in a tragic automobile accident when Elissa was just twelve.

Her grandmother was a no-nonsense kind of lady who dished out priceless wisdom with brutally honest insights. It was the same way she dished out huge bowls of pasta with her amazing meatballs and homemade sauce. Not to mention a side order of back-breaking hugs that Elissa still missed.

Nonna cooked like that all the time. She made a huge pot of sauce every weekend, and she was happy to serve it to Elissa and her teammates and friends, especially after games and tournaments.

Soccer had been her sport of choice, and cooking had soon become her favorite hobby. Her grandmother had encouraged her in both pursuits. Guiding her in one and cheering her on in the other. Elissa still missed her terribly.

"Hey babe, ain't you gonna eat nothin'? You know they charge twenty dollars just to sit down," Little Gianni interrupted her train of thought.

Elissa was forced to turn her mind back to the present, which unfortunately included watching, *and hearing*, him as he sucked on his teeth and stuffed another breaded shrimp down his throat.

"I'm fine," she answered with a polite smile plastered on her face.

Just get home, Lissa. Just get him to take you home.

Elissa closed her eyes when he looked back down at his dish. Thank God for small favors, she mused. At least he was more interested in eating at the moment.

He'd taken her to the rattiest looking hotel and casino she'd ever seen in her life. And the buffet room?

Ew.

Seriously, the place had to be violating at least a dozen health codes. When Gianni had said Atlantic City, she'd thought at least the atmosphere would be exciting. But they were so far from the real glitz and entertainment, they might as well be anywhere else.

She sighed, looking at the plate she'd made for herself. Elissa couldn't even fake an interest in the food. As a chef, it was hard enough to dine out.

She was always judging the food, the service, the ingredients. How could she not? It was her business. And that was when the food was good!

This was not good. Not at all.

She'd been to hospitals that served better food. Old yellow lights buzzed and blinked around the buffet, giving it an abandoned kind of feel. The menu was made up of mostly frozen then fried or baked cuisine.

Reheated actually. It was like a giant TV dinner buffet where every item was previously frozen when already cooked and warmed up in an oven.

It was the kind of food sold cheap at restaurant supply stores in bulk. Yeah, this was much worse than hospital food, in her opinion.

There was a worn carpet on the floor, a handful of scattered tables in the dining room, elevator music on in the background, and the entire place smelled like canned soup.

Not to mention not one of the five people there besides them was under sixty years old.

"Gianni," she said, leaning forward so as not to hurt his feelings.

"I thought you mentioned something about seeing a show tonight. Is it here?"

Please don't be here.

If he was taking her somewhere else, she could beg off and hire a cab to take her home. There was no way she was sitting through anything else with this man. Not now. Not ever.

"Ah, I see, babe, you want some entertainment first, I get it," he snickered loudly, and she blanched.

Whatever he thought was going to happen wasn't. She needed to disabuse him of the notion, and fast.

"Alright, alright. Lemme finish this, babe. Then we'll go up to the room I got for us," he said.

Before she could make sense of the ludicrous statement, he slurped another fried shrimp, don't ask how. Then he grabbed her arm and yanked her from the seat before she could even react.

Elissa tugged on his hold, but the man was immovable. Tossing a five-dollar bill on the table, Little Gianni snatched a toothpick from the hostess stand before dragging her outside.

Great, he was a cheap tipper, too.

All she wanted was to go home. Figuring the best way to do that would probably be to get him to the car, she let him lead the way.

Once inside, she would ask him to drive back to Hoboken so she could wring Gretchen's neck. Fuming, she pulled her arm out of his hand and walked behind him.

The rain was really pouring, and the cheap bastard had refused valet. Elissa ducked her head so she wouldn't get so wet. Of course, the jacket she'd brought was light and had no hood.

Gianni had an umbrella, but he didn't offer to hold it for her, and honestly, she did not relish the idea of getting any closer to him than necessary.

Seriously, not happening.

Now all she had to do was break the news. She had no intention of watching a show or returning to the hotel with him.

What could go wrong?

Grab your copy at https://www.cdgorri.com/books/ purrfectly-mated!

About the Author

C.D. Gorri is a USA Today Bestselling author of steamy paranormal romance and urban fantasy. She is the creator of the Grazi Kelly Universe.

Join her mailing list here: https://www.cdgorri.com/newsletter

An avid reader with a profound love for books and literature, when she is not writing or taking care of her family, she can usually be found with a book or tablet in hand. C.D. lives in her home state of New Jersey where many of her characters or stories are based. Her tales are fast paced yet detailed with satisfying conclusions.

If you enjoy powerful heroines and loyal heroes who face relatable problems in supernatural settings, journey into the Grazi Kelly Universe today. You will find sassy, curvy heroines and sexy, love-driven heroes who find their HEAs between the pages. Werewolves, Bears, Dragons, Tigers, Witches, Romani, Lynxes, Foxes, Thunderbirds, Vampires, and many more Shifters and supernatural creatures dwell within her worlds. The most important thing is every mate in this universe is fated, loyal, and true lovers always get their happily ever afters.

Want to know how it all began? Enter the Grazi Kelly Universe with Wolf Moon: A Grazi Kelly Novel or pick up Charley's Christmas Wolf and dive into the Macconwood Pack Novel Series today.

For a complete list of C.D. Gorri's books visit her website here:

https://www.cdgorri.com/complete-book-list/

Thank you and happy reading!

del mare alla stella,
    C.D. Gorri

Follow C.D. Gorri here:
    http://www.cdgorri.com

https://www.facebook.com/Cdgorribooks
https://www.bookbub.com/authors/c-d-gorri
https://twitter.com/cgor22
https://instagram.com/cdgorri/
https://www.goodreads.com/cdgorri
https://www.tiktok.com/@cdgorriauthor

Ingram Content Group UK Ltd.
Milton Keynes UK
UKHW020804190723
425424UK00017B/289